"Why'd you go chasing after 'em?" Jeremy screamed.

"Didn't you see I was ready to shoot?"

"I saw buffalo hightailing it away from us!" James yelled back. "They smelled you just like I said they would!"

The brothers kept shouting for another fifteen minutes, blaming each other for the day's lost meal. Finally they grew tired of hollering and trudged toward camp in silence, each hating the other.

As they neared the wagons, however, they put aside their disagreement.

Pa was not in the wagon. He was stretched across the ground. A man stood over him, while another man held Ma by the arm. The two men were carrying rifles, and they had them pointed at their prisoners.

James and Jeremy dove behind a tangle of sage to avoid being spotted.

"Desperadoes!" James whispered.

Don't miss the other two books in this exciting western trilogy:

Across the Wild River

Over the Rugged Mountain *

from HarperPaperbacks!

*coming soon

ALONG THE DANGEROUS TRAIL

BILL GUTMAN

HarperPaperbacks

A Division of HarperCollins*Publishers*

HarperPaperbacks *A Division of* HarperCollins*Publishers*
10 East 53rd Street, New York, N.Y. 10022

Copyright © 1993 by Daniel Weiss Associates, Inc.

Cover art copyright © 1993 Daniel Weiss Associates, Inc.

All rights reserved. No part of this book may be used or reproduced in any manner whatsoever without written permission of the publisher, except in the case of brief quotations embodied in critical articles and reviews. For information address Daniel Weiss Associates, Inc., 33 West 17th Street, New York, New York 10011.

Produced by Daniel Weiss Associates, Inc., 33 West 17th Street, New York, New York 10011.

First printing: November, 1993

Printed in the United States of America

HarperPaperbacks and colophon are trademarks of HarperCollins*Publishers*

10 9 8 7 6 5 4 3 2 1

Along The Dangerous Trail

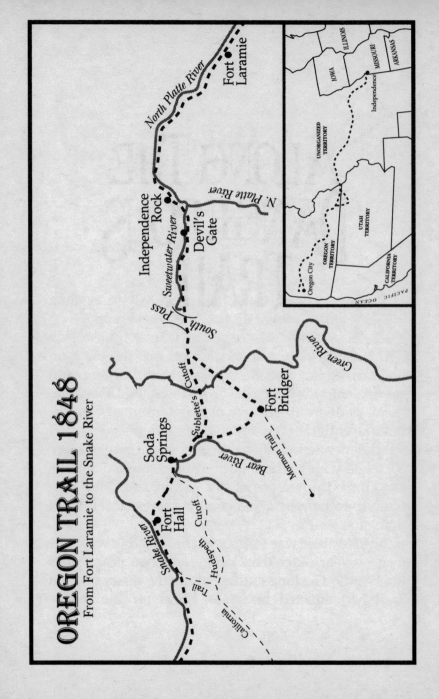

OREGON TRAIL 1848

From Fort Laramie to the Snake River

ONE

FORT LARAMIE

"**H**urry up, Cady," called James Gregg, tugging at the brim of his hat. "Let's get going."

James was eager to take a look inside Fort Laramie. The wagon train he was traveling on had arrived just outside the walls that morning, and set up camp for the day. The fort was the first settlement, aside from a couple of small trading outposts, that the emigrants on the train had seen since they'd left Independence, Missouri, over seven weeks ago.

"Hold your horses!" Cady Walker shouted. Finally she jumped down out of her wagon and came running up to James. "I was checking on Scott. He's not doing too well."

Scott Walker was Cady's big brother. He was thirteen—a year older than James, and two years older than Cady. The long journey along the dusty Oregon Trail had affected his weak lungs for the worse.

1

Now, most of the time, he was too sickly even to leave his family's wagon.

"Sorry to hear that," James said. He wondered if he should go see how Scott was, but then thought better of it. Mrs. Walker would be in the wagon with him. James wasn't fond of talking to her. She was a harsh, pinched woman.

"I've been waiting for you all morning," James went on. "Pa and Jeremy left an hour ago." Jeremy was James's older brother.

"You could've gone to the fort without me," Cady replied. "I wasn't stopping you. But I reckon you needed someone like me to show you around." She sighed dramatically.

"Hardly." James rolled his eyes. He knew Cady prided herself on being from Philadelphia. But being from a city didn't mean she would know her way around a busy fort. She just wanted him to think so.

James was from a farm outside the little town of Franklin, Pennsylvania. He'd been overwhelmed by the crowds and bustle of Independence.

They started toward the fort. The blue sky arched over their heads and the flat, dusty land around them shimmered with the heat. Like a lone ship at sea, the whitewashed adobe-brick fort shone against the brown of the plains.

Fort Laramie was a low, rectangular two-story structure with three blockhouses—two at opposite corners and the third over the gate in the front wall.

The fort had been built by the American Fur Company. The U.S. Army had little authority on the frontier—American Fur Company agents ruled Fort Laramie like a private state.

Camped outside the fort was a group of Dakota Indians. They were tall and wore buffalo robes about their waists, but no paint. Their long black hair was pulled back and fixed in place with eagle feathers.

James had gotten used to seeing Indians along the trail. His family had traded with the Potawatomi, and he, Cady, and Scott had even been saved from wolves by some Pawnees. But he was surprised to see Indians living so close to whites. Then he remembered his pa had told him they were there to trade with the trappers, soldiers, and emigrants who passed through the fort.

James and Cady walked through the first of the two wide wooden gates. On the right was a little window in the adobe wall. Through it the people inside the fort could conduct business with the Indians while still keeping the inner gate closed. Usually both gates were kept open, though, and Indians came and went freely.

Inside, the fort was as crowded as Independence. There were blacksmiths and wheelwrights, trappers and traders. James and Cady couldn't believe the prices. A pound of flour cost fifty cents, as did a gross of fishhooks. Coffee, sugar, and salt were a dollar a pound.

What seemed like dozens of languages flew back and forth. Besides the fur company agents, soldiers, and emigrants who spoke English, there were Indians of every description, each using a different tongue, Mexicans talking in Spanish, and traders calling in French.

An elderly Oglala Indian offered pemmican—dried buffalo meat ground up with berries, fat, and marrow. A Brulé Indian was hawking kinnikinnick, a variety of tobacco, and shongsasha, the bark of the red willow, also used for smoking.

Lining the walls of the fort were little rooms. Some were horse stables, and others, mostly on the second story, were the quarters of the fur company agents. Inside many of the lower rooms sat Indian women idly fanning at the dust and flies that choked the air.

Suddenly a commotion sprang up not far from where James and Cady were looking at a pair of beaded moccasins a Dakota wanted to trade. Quickly they made their way over to a crowd of men gathered in a corner of the yard. A number of them were shouting angrily and shaking their fists.

"What's all the fuss?" Cady asked James.

"Don't know," he answered. "Wait here." He recognized Mr. Teague, from the train, among the men and sidled up to him.

"Mornin', Mr. Teague," James greeted him. "What're those men shouting about?"

"Why, howdy, James," said Mr. Teague. "Seems they caught the'selves a desperado in the Black Hills. That man over yonder." He pointed into the crowd. "They say he's been rustling horses. Him and his gang, the Clampson boys."

"Land's sake . . ." James murmured. A real desperado. Back in Pennsylvania, he'd read stories about outlaws in the penny papers, but he never thought he'd see one. He stood on tiptoe and tried to peer over the backs of the men.

"They say the Clampson boys is bloody murderous," Mr. Teague continued. "There's three more of 'em. Shot some poor feller dead just afore we hitched out. In Independence."

"Independence?" James repeated. He'd seen a shooting there. He'd fairly stepped over the wounded man.

"So they say." Mr. Teague nodded. "Though it warn't this one, but his brother Tom that done it."

"What're they going to do with him?" James asked.

"Oh," Mr. Teague chuckled, "them fellers'll invite him to a necktie party, I reckon."

James was about to ask Mr. Teague what he meant by a necktie party, but he'd disappeared into the crowd. So James trotted back to Cady, who was trying to get a look at the goings-on, and repeated what Mr. Teague had told him. "What's a necktie party?" he concluded.

5

"A necktie party!" Cady whooped. "You don't know what a necktie party is? Hoo, you oughta thank your stars I know something about the world!"

James waited while Cady finished laughing. "All right, smarty," he said at last. "If you know so much, what *is* a necktie party?"

"A hanging!" Cady smirked. "If you weren't so blamed ignorant, you'd know that."

"Well, if you weren't so blamed ignorant," James retorted, "you'd know how to swim. I'm getting tired of saving your life all the time."

That calmed Cady right down. "Hmph," she said. "I can swim plenty. Just not in water over my head."

James laughed. "The river was only four feet deep, and you nearly drowned in it." He waved his arms over his head. "Glug, glug, help me, help me," he teased.

It was true. Cady had nearly drowned in the raging waters of the South Platte River. James had risked his own life to rescue her.

Cady wrinkled up her face. "Never mind my swimming. Let's go watch the hanging. I hear tell they're mighty good entertainment." She grabbed his sleeve and led him toward the crowd.

The men were now gathered near a corner blockhouse. The blockhouse roof jutted past the fort's walls, extending into the yard at a height of about fifteen feet. Someone had tossed a rope over one of the roof's rafters. At the end of the rope dangled a noose.

6

James swallowed, and felt a tingling at the back of his neck. He sure wouldn't want that noose tied around him.

James could see the desperado now. The angry men had tied his hands behind his back and propped him up on a horse. He was a large man, with a long, narrow, bony face and deep-set eyes. By the looks of him, he hadn't had a meal in days. His clothes were raggedy and ill-fitting, as if they'd been made for someone else, but his boots were shiny new. James shivered at the thought of where he'd gotten them—off a dead man's feet, no doubt.

Cady hadn't let go of his sleeve since she'd dragged him over here, and now her fingers crept down around his own. He glanced over at her. She was staring at the proceedings with an open mouth.

A man had climbed up on a barrel and was making a speech about how, as a representative of the American Fur Company, he was the law in these parts, and how he wasn't tolerating no horse-thieving scoundrels of any color.

James remembered a similar scene. A man in their wagon train, Jenson Carver, had shot and killed an Indian unprovoked. The emigrants had decided to hand him over to the Pawnees rather than risk reprisal. James knew that despite this man's claims to be in charge, the will of the crowd was law on the frontier.

Swiftly the man on the barrel slipped the noose

over the desperado's head. Someone else pulled the slack out of the rope and secured it to a hitching post.

Cady's grip on James's hand tightened.

"Yah!" the man on the barrel yelled, slapping the horse hard on the rear and leaping down from the barrel. The horse lunged forward a few steps, and the desperado tumbled off its back.

The desperado arched his body and kicked out his legs two or three times, swinging his bound arms behind his back. But the thrashing seemed only to tighten the noose around his neck.

He stopped kicking, and threw his head back tensely and gasped for air. A tight grimace creased his face. He was dangling three feet off the ground. His eyes blinked slowly in the noonday sun.

James's hand ached now, Cady was squeezing it so tight. But he paid it no mind. He was too caught up in the desperado's struggle for life.

The desperado made soft coughing noises between his clenched teeth. Gurgling noises rose from his throat. He started kicking again, thrashing around wildly, as if he were trying to swim in air. His body arched from the back of his head all the way down to his heels, then went limp. His face was a dark, dark red and was turning blue fast. He arched again, gurgling horribly.

James felt sick to his stomach. He'd seen men wounded before, but he'd never actually watched one die. He hadn't known how awful it would be.

Now, too, his hand was hurting him badly. Cady's nails were digging into his skin. He looked at her. A tear was running down her freckled cheek, and she looked pale. James regretted watching the necktie party. He wanted to leave. But somehow he couldn't help staying till the last dance was done.

The desperado arched one more time and went limp. His head flopped forward, chin on collarbone, tongue on lower lip. He blinked ever so slowly, once, twice, and then his eyes stared ahead dully, seeing nothing, saying nothing.

It was over.

TWO

HELP YOURSELF

They returned to the emigrant camp in low spirits. For all Cady's talk of how much fun necktie parties were, she was deeply troubled by what she'd seen.

"How could they just hang him like that, James?" she wailed. "Stringing him up like a dog! Worse'n a dog." She shivered. "It was horrible."

"He had it coming," James asserted, though he doubted his words. "He was a bad man."

"I don't know about that. You said it was his brother who shot the man in Independence."

"But he rustled horses, and that's a capital offense, punishable by death. Anyway, what's done's done. Just don't invite me to any more necktie parties."

"I won't, believe you me."

James and Cady approached the Greggs' wagon. James's ma and pa, brother Jeremy, and sister Eliza-

10

beth were gathered round a small campfire. Ma was fixing fried corn cakes and roast antelope. Pa had shot the antelope that morning. James's mouth watered at the smell of the meat cooking. It had been a long day.

"Why, Cady," Ma said, "sit down here and have some supper with us." She patted the dusty ground beside her.

"Thank you, ma'am," Cady said, plopping down. Cady had begun eating most of her meals with the Greggs. It took so much of her mother's energy to nurse Scott that often she was too weary to make supper.

Besides, Mrs. Walker herself felt ill almost every morning. Some days she was so sick, she didn't leave the wagon at all. She would sit in the front, reading the Bible aloud to Scott. And Mr. Walker had his hands full driving and caring for the team of four oxen.

James's ma had taken to fixing a little extra supper and slipping off to the Walker wagon with it. Mr. and Mrs. Walker and Scott always appreciated the food.

James and Cady loaded their tin plates with strips of smoking meat and corn cakes.

"I never relished victuals so well," James said with his mouth full.

"Me neither," said Cady.

Ma smiled approvingly and put another cake on each of their plates.

11

James felt like there was nothing better in the world than a hot meal eaten outdoors. At times, he wished the trail would go on forever. But in his heart, he knew he would be glad to finally reach Oregon City, stake out some land with his parents, and start up a farm.

"I talked to some interesting traders at the fort today," Jeremy said enthusiastically. "They were coming from out west. Said gold's been found in the California hills." Jeremy was fifteen. He had not wanted to leave his sweetheart in Pennsylvania. But after saving his pa's life in a buffalo stampede, he seemed happier about life on the trail.

"That so?" Pa said without much interest.

"Yep," Jeremy went on. "Man name of Sutter. In a creek, last January. He tried to keep it quiet, but a secret like that won't keep. They say the nuggets are just lying on the ground, big as your fist."

"All you have to do is pick 'em up?" Elizabeth asked. She was only six.

"That's right." Jeremy nodded. "And stuff 'em in your pockets."

"My!" Elizabeth said. She looked down at her checkered linsey-woolsey dress. "I'd need deeper pockets!"

Jeremy chuckled and ruffled her hair. "Mine are deep enough for both of us."

"Hardly seems fair," Pa said thoughtfully. "Gold on the ground in California, and us going to Oregon. We're gonna have to clear trees, plow, sow, and reap before we get any gold out of the ground." He smiled, and winked at James. "But we will. You can be sure of that. We will."

"I was thinking," Jeremy said quietly, "that maybe, after we get to Oregon, I'd just head on down to California." He studied his now-empty tin plate. "Just to see if what they say is true."

The group was silent. James stared at Jeremy. How could he plan on abandoning the family like that? They would need him in Oregon as much as they'd needed him on the trail. If it weren't for him, Pa would have been killed. Surely Jeremy must know how much they depended on him.

Finally Pa said, "We'll discuss that when the time comes, son. In the meanwhile, why don't you help me water the animals and tie them up for the night." He and Jeremy left the campfire.

James looked at his ma. Tears welled in her eyes as she gathered the plates.

Early the next morning Colonel Stewart, the trail boss, ordered the wagons into the usual train.

The colonel and Pierre Delaroux, a French trapper who'd been hired as a guide, took the lead. Behind them came the eighteen wagons. The Greggs were about midway in the train, behind the widow Loughery and in front of the Walkers.

James walked alongside his family's wagon, helping his pa drive the pair of oxen. After a while he dropped back to check on Bolt, his young horse.

Bolt had been a sickly colt, and his owner, Eli Meacham, was going to put him down. When James offered to take him, Mr. Meacham agreed. Under James's care, Bolt had gotten stronger, and Mr. Meacham had tried to reclaim him. But James's friend Will Gantry had persuaded Mr. Meacham that it would be unwise to try to cheat James. Bolt belonged to him fair and square.

"You're looking mighty good, boy," James said, slapping Bolt on the withers.

Bolt nickered and shook his head, prancing lively.

James was amazed at how healthy Bolt looked. When he'd first seen him, Bolt was all bones. Now his shoulders bulged with flesh, and his chest and haunches had filled out. His speckled gray coat had a glossy sheen, and even his whinny sounded deeper.

James couldn't wait to ride him. Bolt was still young and hadn't been broken, but James knew he was almost ready. Occasionally James took a saddle off of Corncob or Mackie, the family's other two horses, and placed it on Bolt's back for the day. Bolt trusted James, and never shied under the saddle.

James reached up and scratched Bolt behind the ear. "Soon we'll be flying over the plains together, just you and me," he whispered.

Bolt nickered in agreement.

Just then Will Gantry came riding up on his big black steed. He swung down gracefully to the ground.

"Will," James hailed him. "Where's Sara?"

Sara was Will's wife. She'd been traveling with her parents, the Jenningtons. Will and Sara'd met on the trail and been married only the week before.

"She's with her family." Will motioned toward the rear of the train. "Mr. Jenning—I mean, Father has her watching the cows."

James snickered at Will's forcing himself to call Mr. Jennington "Father." James wondered what Will's folks were like.

"Say, Will," he said, "what made you light out for Oregon, anyway? Didn't you like Virginia?" James's family had left Pennsylvania because their little farm couldn't support them. But Will had come from a big plantation.

"Oh, I love Virginia," Will replied. "It's the prettiest state in the Union." Then his face darkened. "But there are . . . uh, aspects of life in the Old Dominion I couldn't abide."

"You mean slavery?" James asked.

There were no slaves in Pennsylvania, where James grew up. But Virginia still maintained the "peculiar institution." James's ma had raised him to believe human bondage was un-Christian. He had seen some slaves working the ferries in Missouri. That was enough to convince him it was a sin.

"That's right, Jamie." Will peered up at the sky. "But my daddy doesn't see eye-to-eye with me on that. The time came for me to leave. So I did."

15

"I'm sorry for that."

"I am, too, Jamie. My daddy's a good man, but he can't see where the future is. Slavery's ending. People won't stand for it, and not just Yankees. I'm talking about Southerners, too. They'll understand how it's wrong. In fifteen years, every man in America will be free."

"I hope you're right," said James.

"I am, you'll see." Will jumped back up on his horse. "I best be going. Delaroux wanted me to help him scout out routes. We'll be in the Black Hills before the week's out." Will waved and galloped off.

James watched him ride west. Ahead of him, the pale peaks of the Rocky Mountains were already in sight.

Two days later the train entered the red-earth country of the Black Hills. The wagons were still moving up the south bank of the North Platte, as they had been for hundreds of miles. But now the flat plains were giving way to rocky gulches and jutting ridges.

The trail wove around and over hills and crags, splitting apart at times, the different strands later rejoining. Some routes simply came upon dead ends. It was in this territory that an experienced guide like Pierre Delaroux was most needed.

Steep grades were new to the emigrants, and to the animals. James's pa had to use the whip more often on the oxen than he had since the very start of the trip. Still, he never actually hit them with it. A good sharp crack over their heads was enough to keep them moving.

James and Jeremy were kept busy helping their pa with the team. They also ran back and forth along the train, pushing other families' wagons over crests and pulling them out of ditches.

The discarded property at the side of the road, James noticed, was coming in bunches now. The trail all the way back to Independence had been littered here and there with trunks, chairs, and tables. But now, in the first hills, people unloaded everything that wasn't absolutely essential.

Mahogany dressers blistered in the sun and dust. Intricately carved grandfather clocks, beautiful floor mirrors, settees, rolled-up rugs, and boxes inlaid with mother-of-pearl lay in heaps by the trail. One stack even had a hand-painted sign on top that said HELP YOURSELF.

No one did. The emigrants knew that whatever they picked up now, they'd just have to ditch later.

James's ma had left a chest of drawers way back on the banks of the Big Blue River. His pa had sold an iron anvil at Fort Laramie just to be rid of it.

James headed back to check on the Walkers. Even though they had four oxen, compared to the Greggs' two, they were having a hard time with the grades. Mrs. Walker refused to shed any of her possessions.

This—plus the fact that she and Scott had to ride in the wagon, as they were too ill to walk—made their wagon extremely heavy.

James waved to Mr. Walker, who was driving his oxen, and waited for the wagon to come up to him.

Cady was walking behind the wagon, giving it a hard shove every two or three steps.

"You can't push it all the way to Oregon," James remarked.

Cady shot him a look. "I may have to," she said, puffing at her bangs, which kept flapping into her eyes.

James fell in step beside her and commenced shoving the wagon.

"James," came a feeble voice from inside the wagon. "How you doing? Haven't seen you in a while."

"Scott?" James squinted into the darkness of the rolling wagon. He made out a small, pale figure stretched out beneath a table. "What're you doing under there?"

"It's the only place there's room enough for me to lie down," Scott said hoarsely. He broke into a wheezing cough.

James was shocked. He knew his friend was sick, but he hadn't realized how serious it was. Now that his eyes were accustomed to the darkness of the wagon's interior, he saw that Scott had noticeably shrunk over the last few weeks. His fingers were like bones, and his face had lost its healthy roundness.

"Where's your ma?" James asked.

"Up front." Scott motioned over his shoulder. "Asleep. She sleeps a lot these days."

Cady grunted as she shoved the wagon forward.

"Hmm," said James. Cady smacked her hands against the back of the wagon and groaned with the effort of pushing.

It wasn't fair, James thought. Mrs. Walker was riding comfortably while her daughter worked like an animal. Wasn't walking all the way to Oregon enough, without having to push a wagon, too?

"Why are you doing this to yourself?" he whispered to Cady.

Cady puffed at her bangs and slapped the wagon again. "James," she said testily, "Scott and Mother aren't well. I have to do my share."

"You're doing more than your share, seems to me."

She said nothing, just dug in her heels and kept pushing.

"No wonder you're so stubborn," James said, trying to goad her into an argument. "The way you're working, you must be half mule."

Cady ignored him.

Finally James could stand it no longer. He ran around to the front of the wagon. "You know Cady's back there pushing, don't you?" he shouted at Mr. Walker.

Mr. Walker stopped clucking at the weary oxen, and they halted immediately.

"How's that, Jamie?" he asked.

19

"I said Cady's beating herself up to keep you going while other people are napping!"

"Cady's doing *what*?" Mr. Walker dropped the whip and ran to the back of the wagon. James followed him.

"Cady, land's sake, what do you think you're doing back here?" Mr. Walker asked her. "I thought you were right behind me."

Cady shrugged. "Wagon won't make it 'less I help out." She held up her hands. They were blistered red from shoving the rough wood.

Mr. Walker stared at her hands, then took them in his own. He touched the palms gently. "Oh, my darling girl," he whispered, "you're wearing yourself to the bone!"

Then James saw something he never thought he'd see. Mr. Walker, a grown man, picked Cady up, clasped her to his chest, and burst into tears. "I'm sorry, honey, I'm sorry," he wailed into her neck.

"You didn't do anything," Cady replied. She seemed as astonished as James was.

"You're right, Cady. I didn't do anything. And it's about time I did." Mr. Walker set her down, wiping his eyes. "Rebecca!" he bellowed into the wagon. "Wake up, woman! We're gonna have us a spring cleaning."

James, Cady, and Mr. Walker made quite an impressive mountain out of Mrs. Walker's stuff. There were three trunks, two big tables, two heavy chairs, a wooden bed frame, a wardrobe, five small boxes,

20

and, last but certainly not least, a spinet, which was a kind of small upright piano.

James wondered how it had all fit in the wagon in the first place.

"Wasn't easy," Cady said.

Mr. Walker allowed his wife to keep her writing desk. "I know it's important to you," he offered.

She just pursed her lips and climbed back into the wagon.

Mr. Walker made Cady rest with her mother and Scott all that day and most of the next.

THREE

THE GLORIOUS FOURTH

Colonel Stewart had hoped to reach Independence Rock, a large landmark near the banks of the Sweetwater River, by the Fourth of July. But a slow start, coupled with a dust storm in the third week of June, had put the train a little behind schedule.

After the dust storm, the emigrants had made good time, averaging about fifteen miles a day, even over the rough terrain of the Black Hills. Though the country was rough, it was a hunter's paradise. The hills were filled with gray hares, white-tailed antelope, elk, black-tailed deer, and even the occasional bighorn sheep. Plus, the kings of the prairie, the buffaloes, and their court jesters, the groundhogs, were still in abundance.

Except for one day stuck in the dust storm, the emigrants had moved every day since leaving Missouri in early May. Seven days a week they'd traveled, even on the Sabbath.

22

Now, two days after Mr. Walker had lightened his wagon, Colonel Stewart decided the train could afford to observe the Fourth of July with a day of rest and a small celebration. The emigrants were happy to go along with his idea.

They camped not far from the North Platte. A mile to the south, the colonel said, was a bridge made out of rock.

James's ma started the holiday by sending James, Jeremy, and Elizabeth down to the river to wash.

"Why can't we go see the rock bridge, Ma?" James asked.

"You may," Ma replied. "*After* you're good and clean. Not a one of you has bathed since we left Missouri."

"That's not true," James pointed out. "I went swimming in the South Platte, remember?"

"The South Platte!" Ma laughed. "Why, that river was dirtier than you were! Now get a move on, you rascals. And Jeremy, keep an eye on your sister. When you three get back, I'm sending your pa and myself."

After a good dunking and scrubbing, James went to find Cady and Scott. They were sitting with their parents. Mrs. Walker was reading loudly from the Bible.

"'Behold,'" she declaimed, "'the name of the Lord cometh from far, burning with His anger, and the burden thereof is heavy. . . .'"

James didn't even stop to ask if Cady and Scott could come with him to see the bridge. He knew what the answer would be.

Mrs. Walker was a hard, ungenerous woman, severe with Cady and Scott and unforgiving of others. She even looked pinched and scrawny, though James had noticed that she'd been looking a little plumper around the middle lately. She hated the West. She saw nothing but evil in the land, and she always found words in the Bible to back her up.

But when James's ma read the very same book, she found words that spoke of fruitful trees and cedars, and oliveyards in abundance. James wasn't sure if this said something about the way people were, or the way Scripture was. Probably both, he decided.

James kicked at a rock and headed over toward the Jenningtons' wagon. Maybe Will and Sara would take a look at the bridge with him.

Sara was sitting on a low crate, mending the canvas top of her family's "prairie schooner."

James flumped on the ground next to her and crossed his legs. He plucked a weed and put it between his teeth. "Whatcha doin'?"

"Sewing." Sara smiled. Her thick mess of black hair was tied back with a bright red ribbon. She wiggled her eyebrows at him. "What *choo* doin'?"

"Nothing." James tossed the weed away. It was bitter. "I wanted to go see the rock bridge Colonel

Stewart told us about, but I can't find anyone to go with me."

"Where's Cady?"

"Oh, her ma's yammerin' away at her about heavy burdens and stuff. You know."

Sara's face went serious. "James, you should try to be more understanding of Mrs. Walker. She's not as strong as some others."

"I know she's sick, but that doesn't . . ." James didn't finish. He couldn't go on, not with Sara's big brown eyes looking at him that way.

"Mrs. Walker's not a bad person, Jamie," Sara said softly. "I will admit she tends to look on the bleak side of things, but she is carrying some heavy burdens."

"We all have our troubles," James muttered.

"Now, Jamie," said Sara. "I know you're better than that."

James met her eye. She was gazing at him kindly. He noticed the light brown freckles that dotted her nose and cheekbones. They were like Cady's freckles, only . . . more grown-up or something. He couldn't say. He looked at her thick eyelashes and pretty mouth, then glanced away shyly.

"You know Scott's health worries her," Sara continued. James had to think quick to remember what she was talking about. "And Cady is always getting into scrapes. And now she has another one on the way."

"Huh?" James said.

25

"Didn't you know?" Sara shook her head. "I just hope we make it to Oregon City before the little one comes."

James was still trying to take in the knowledge that Mrs. Walker was expecting when he spied Will sneaking up behind Sara. Will put his finger to his mouth, motioning James to hush.

"Ho there, Mrs. Gantry!" Will said as he wrapped his arms around Sara.

"Ouch!" she yelped. "Heavens, Will, look what you made me do." She held up the index finger of her left hand. A small bead of scarlet was forming at the tip, where she'd poked it with her sewing needle.

"I'm sorry, darling," Will said, genuinely abashed. "Let me kiss it and make it better." He pressed her finger to his lips and smooched it, then started nibbling on it gently.

"Stop that, silly!" Sara giggled, and yanked her hand away. James knew he was blushing as fiercely as she was.

"I don't like to see my beautiful flower hurt," Will said, cuddling her.

"No harm done." She smiled at Will and kissed him lightly on the nose. "Just don't sneak up on me when I'm sewing."

James knew Will was about the luckiest man alive. Sara was so forgiving, and kind, and sweet. Not to mention pretty. Suddenly James felt hot all over.

26

He stood up. "I best be going. Pa might need me for something."

"What, I come along and you have to scamper?" Will teased.

"Didn't you want to go up and see the rock bridge?" Sara asked. "Maybe Will would go with you."

James grinned at her. She was thinking of him! "Naw, I don't care about any old rocks. I'm too old for that." He spun on his heels and ran off, leaving Will and Sara shaking their heads in bewilderment.

On the way back to his wagon, James repeated the name Sara over and over. It was about the prettiest name he'd ever heard.

In the evening the emigrants celebrated the Glorious Fourth. Men fired off guns, and everyone feasted on a buffalo that Pierre Delaroux had shot that morning.

After the last plate was licked clean, and the last song sung, and the last reel danced, everyone gathered in a field. They stood at attention facing east, toward their beloved country so recently left behind, while Colonel Stewart read aloud the Declaration of Independence.

James was next to Cady. Behind him and to his left, about twenty feet away, were Will and Sara. He couldn't help glancing over his shoulder at her. The sun setting threw an orange halo all around her. Just like an angel, James thought.

27

Finally Cady stomped on his foot and told him to stop squirming. "She's too old for you," she hissed. "And besides, Will got to her first."

James pretended he didn't know what she was talking about. To make it up to her, though, he took hold of her hand. He was surprised, and a little pleased, that she didn't pull it away.

When the colonel read "'. . . with a firm reliance on the protection of Divine Providence, we mutually pledge to each other our lives, our fortunes, and our sacred honor,'" many of the assembled were sniffing back tears.

They knew the words applied to themselves as much as they ever had to the Founding Fathers who'd penned them.

Four

INDEPENDENCE ROCK

The emigrants saw the last of the North Platte a few days later, crossing it by way of the Mormon Ferry, which had been established the year before by Brigham Young. They were charged two dollars a wagon for the service. The price was steep, but as Colonel Stewart pointed out, it was cheaper than losing all your possessions in the river.

Waving good riddance to the North Platte, the emigrants climbed up and down a high pass, and the next day struck west across a sandy desert. The only water to be found was in alkali springs. The springs burbled out of the ground as a yellowish creamy fluid with a white crust around the edges. James didn't think they looked very refreshing. When one of Mr. Smoot's oxen wandered off the trail, drank from one, and died not six hours later, James was glad he hadn't partaken of any.

Finally, after a fourteen-hour dash across the desert, the train reached Willow Springs. The emigrants watered their animals, refilled their canteens, and camped beneath a stand of cottonwood, ash, and spruce trees.

Night fell fast and cold in the foothills of the Rockies. James had walked every step of the way across the desert, much of it behind the Walkers' wagon. He'd wanted to keep poor Scott company. Now James was bone tired.

He curled up in his blanket and watched the stars blink in and out behind the swaying branches of a cottonwood. His mind drifted with the gentle breeze. He thought of Sara, and of Cady, and of Scott. . . . Would Scott ever get well?

Before James could contemplate the disturbing question further, he was sound asleep.

The next morning James was walking with Cady. Ever since her pa had lightened the wagon, Cady had stopped trying to push it. They were shuffling along not talking about anything.

Occasionally one of them would point out a curlew overhead, or a jackrabbit hiding in the brush, or a patch of gooseberries by the side of the trail. Miles would go by, though, with neither of them saying anything. But it was nice for the company, anyway.

Suddenly Cady shouted, "Look!" and broke into

a run. The trail was rounding a low ridge. James sprinted after her. Beyond the ridge, a good ten miles away, lay Independence Rock.

"Take a look at that," James murmured, then whistled lowly.

Even from this distance, Independence Rock was impressive. A huge smooth stone dropped down in the middle of a flat sage plain, the rock looked like an immense loaf of bread. Its dark gray, almost black color contrasted sharply with the dusty green all around it.

"I hope Scott'll feel strong enough to climb it with us," Cady said.

"We'll scratch his name in for him if he's not." James knew it was a tradition for emigrants to carve their names, and the year, in the rock. For weeks he'd been looking forward to adding his own. Now the famous landmark was finally in sight.

The train halted that afternoon just beyond Independence Rock, on the banks of the Sweetwater River. Even though they were weary from their long journey, the emigrants hurried to circle the wagons and make camp. Everyone wanted to scramble up the rock and scratch a name on its face before the sun set.

James led Bolt down the banks and let him drink. The Sweetwater was a pretty river, sparkling and clean. His pa had told him they'd be traveling up it for over a hundred miles, until they reached the

South Pass of the Rockies and the first waters of the Pacific. It was hard to believe they'd come as far as they already had.

James turned to Jeremy, who was watering Corncob and Mackie. "You suppose you'll ever see Missy again?" he asked. Missy was Jeremy's sweetheart back in Pennsylvania.

"What kind of question is that?" Jeremy said. "Of course I'll see her again."

When they'd started the trip, James hadn't understood how Jeremy could be so worked up about leaving a girl behind. James thought about Will and Sara. Then he thought about just Sara. He was beginning to understand.

"Missy's pretty, isn't she?" James offered. He'd never really thought so, but he reckoned Jeremy would be glad to hear him say it. He was right.

"She's the . . . she's the . . ." Jeremy broke into a wide grin. "She's right pretty, little brother, you bet she is. She's the most beautiful girl in the whole world. And when I'm a millionaire in California, I'm gonna send for her by clipper ship, and we'll get married in San Francisco and have a big house and I'll wear beaver-skin top hats and smoke eight-inch cigars."

James was laughing, and Jeremy started laughing too. "It's true," he went on. "And if you behave yourself, I'll invite you and Cady down to stay with us."

"Me and Cady?" James stopped laughing. "What's that supposed to mean?"

"Oh, nothing," Jeremy said loftily. He batted his eyes at James. "You smooth talker, you."

"Very funny," James muttered, and went back to watering Bolt. But he wasn't too mad. Jeremy was teasing him, but he hadn't meant it in a bad way.

Still, James was troubled. Jeremy seemed awful intent on going to California.

James, Scott, and Cady stood on the summit of Independence Rock. Scott was doubled over, hands on knees, trying to catch his breath. A high whistling like out-of-tune organ pipes came from his chest. James and Cady had had to carry him the last hundred yards or so.

They could see for miles in all directions. In the east, the Sweetwater River coiled off into the approaching darkness. In the west, the river sparkled in the lowering sun and faded into the foothills of the Rockies. Under their feet were names carved into the surface of the rock—emigrants who had come before.

James drew a large nail out of his overalls pocket and held it up. "Here goes," he said, kneeling.

He scratched at the dark gray rock, carefully forming the letters. The rock crumbled easily under the sharp point of the iron nail, and in only a few minutes he'd written:

JAMES GREGG

Then he handed the nail to Cady, and she added her name beneath his. Scott went last. James took the nail, bent down again, and completed the inscription:

JAMES GREGG
CADY WALKER
SCOTT WALKER
1848

"Maybe we'll come back someday and find our names here," said Cady.

"We ought to make a pact," said James. "We'll meet on this spot in fifty years—no, let's make it fifty-two. It'll be 1900. That way we won't forget."

"1900!" said Cady. "I'll be . . . sixty-three."

"You'll be a grandmother," teased James.

"Please," said Cady. "I can't picture that."

Scott brooded while his sister and friend talked of the future. He looked out over the mountains, toward Oregon.

"You'll make the pact with us?" James asked him.

"I don't know," Scott said. "That's a long time from now."

James and Cady exchanged glances.

"Sure it is," said James. "And I know what you're thinking, Scott. But any of us could die any day. There's smallpox, camp fever, typhus. Why, all three of us almost got eaten by wolves."

Scott smiled weakly at the memory.

"But look how far we've come already," James continued. "We have a long way to go, it's true. But I know we'll all make it. I know it," he finished urgently.

"Scott?" Cady whispered. "Come on. Say you'll come back here with me and Jamie when we're old and wrinkled."

Scott gazed out over the mountains. Finally his thin face took on an expression of resolve. "Let's do it," he said. "I'll make the pact with you."

"Good," said James. He put his hand over his heart. "A solemn oath can never be broken."

Scott and Cady held their hands on their chests in the same way. They vowed to return to Independence Rock on the Fourth of July, 1900, then spat together on the black rock to seal it.

The sun had dropped below the horizon, and a chill had come on the air. They started down the rock in silence. James thought about the pact they'd made. He wished he were as certain as he'd tried to sound that they'd all be able to keep it.

FIVE

DEVIL'S GATE

The next morning Colonel Stewart led the emigrants across the Sweetwater. They forded it at a calm, flat stretch just beyond Independence Rock. The men rode horseback, driving the ox teams and steadying the wagons. The oxen simply pulled the wagons through the water.

It wasn't a difficult operation—the Sweetwater was wide and shallow, only three feet at its deepest. Still, fording any river could be dangerous. Cady and James had nearly drowned while fording the South Platte, which was an easy crossing by reputation.

James was standing on the front board of the wagon, watching Pa and Jeremy ride back and forth. They took turns tending the family's oxen and galloping up to the widow Loughery's team. She was driving them from her wagon—and doing a right good job of it, too, James noted. Occasionally Pa or Jeremy would dash back to check on the Walkers.

"Yow, this river's cold!" Jeremy shouted. Splashing through the water on Corncob, he was drenched to the waist.

"Get used to it, my friend." Pierre Delaroux galloped up. "Before we reach the mountains, we will cross the Sweetwater eight more times. And by then every one of us will be . . . how do you say, intimate with her."

"You mean *familiar*, Mr. Delaroux," the widow Loughery called from the wagon ahead. James noticed she was blushing.

"Ah, yes, familiar. Pardon my English, please, madam," Delaroux said, riding up next to her.

"Bien sur," the widow tittered.

"Ah, the madam speaks French!" Delaroux exclaimed. Then he launched into a long string of what James took to be French words spoken at an extremely rapid pace.

The widow Loughery started laughing. "Oh, Mr. Delaroux, do slow down! My French simply isn't what it used to be."

James watched and listened as Delaroux trotted alongside the widow, both of them chatting gaily in French and English.

Well, James thought, it just goes to show there's no telling who's going to hit it off.

*   *   *

Later that day James was walking next to the wagon, patting Bolt and talking softly to him. "Just wait till we get you saddled up," he whispered. "You'll love thundering across the prairie in Oregon." He paused. Did Oregon have prairie? he wondered. "Anyway, we'll sure have us a time when—"

"How are we going to get through *that*?" Elizabeth asked loudly from the wagon.

James looked up. Looming on the horizon was a four-hundred-foot wall of gray rock. Devil's Gate. He'd heard some of the men talking about it earlier. Down the middle of the rock was a narrow slit through which the suddenly violent Sweetwater came shooting down.

How *were* they going to get through it? James had no idea. They'd been following the Sweetwater, crossing from bank to bank, all day. Surely they weren't going to try to scale Devil's Gate.

"We're not going through it, silly," Jeremy said to Elizabeth. "We're going around it."

"Oh." Elizabeth nodded, satisfied.

James was glad she'd asked before he had. He decided to run back to the Walkers' wagon. "Hey, Cady," he called, "did you see Devil's Gate?"

Cady was walking alongside the wagon, making frantic motions for James to hush. He was about to ask her why when she clapped her hand over his mouth. "Keep it down about Devil's Gate, will you?" she hissed. "If Mother finds out that's what

38

it's called, she'll have conniptions. I'll never hear the end of it."

She raised her hand off James's mouth.

"Sorry," he whispered. Then, "Did you see Old Harry's Gate?"

"Very funny. And yes, I've seen it. I could hardly miss it."

"We'll be circling around to the south to get past it," he said, "but I hear there's some rough country ahead."

"Long as I don't have to push that spinet," Cady muttered, "I don't care how rough the country gets."

"Think I'll go tell your ma how much you miss her furniture," he teased.

"Don't you dare," Cady said, cocking back her fist.

James laughed. "Come on, let's go see your pa instead. He might need help getting the team up the grades."

The trail avoided the pounding Sweetwater and the sheer rock face of the gate itself. But it cut close enough to both that the air was wet from misty plumes rising from the bottom of the falls, and the ground underfoot was smooth gray granite. The hooves of the horses and oxen clacked against the bare rock.

"When I shut my eyes," Cady observed, "I can almost imagine we're walking on cobblestoned streets.

Except the air smells of wildflowers instead of soot and sewers," she joked.

Several times James heard men shouting farther up in the train—an ox losing its footing, or a wagon wheel getting stuck in one of the many fissures in the rock. Colonel Stewart was riding up and down the line, barking out orders and encouragement. James knew his pa and Jeremy had their hands full with the wagon. He was glad Delaroux seemed to have taken the widow Loughery under his wing; she was one less worry for James's pa.

James and Cady walked on either side of Mr. Walker's team of four. Mr. Walker was behind them, talking to the animals, telling them to go left or go right. After two long months on the trail, the oxen almost never needed the whip anymore. A mere word from their driver was enough.

The rock dropped away steeply in places. Unpredictably, too. Brush and low, scrawny trees lined the trail, then suddenly dropped off down steep gullies filled with rock chips and branches. James peered over the edge of the fall-offs as he passed them. Some were forty and fifty feet deep. He could hear the faint thundering of the water shooting through Devil's Gate in the distance.

The Walker wagon had just gained the summit and was beginning the descent of the western slope when James heard shouting coming from behind him.

"What's all that about, I wonder," said Cady.

A cold feeling rose up from the pit of James's stomach. "I have a bad feeling about this, Cady." The shouts were rising in pitch, as if a panic was gripping them. James turned to Mr. Walker. "Can you handle 'em from here, sir?"

Mr. Walker nodded, and James took off running for the tail end of the train.

At first he couldn't tell what had happened. Someone was shouting, "Fetch a rope!" Someone else was yelling, "Come back here, ya blamed fool!"

A dozen men and women were crowded around a section of trail. James recognized the spot. A particularly steep and treacherous gully came right up to the edge of the trail there.

James pushed his way through the crowd. What met his eye was horrible. At the bottom of the canyon, forty feet down, was a tipped-over wagon and a team of four all tangled up and bellowing. The wagon's rounded canvas covering and one of its sides were completely stove in, as if the wagon had rolled down the steep slope. Two of the oxen were struggling to right themselves on shattered legs. The other two just lay there, lowing mournfully.

James saw a figure scrambling down the side of the gully, skidding wildly from scraggly bush to blasted tree. It was Will! And then James almost fell over from dizziness as a terrible realization struck him—the wagon was the Jenningtons'.

41

He searched the crowd around him. There was Mr. Jennington, looking pale as a buffalo skull bleached in the sun. There was Mrs. Jennington, biting her hand to keep from crying. But there was no Sara.

"They were walking with me," cried Mrs. Jennington. "She'd just asked Will if he'd like a drink of water. Then she climbed into the wagon to fetch the canteen."

Mrs. Jennington was sobbing now and crying, "Sara, Sara! Dear Lord, have mercy!"

Her husband took her in his arms and held her tight. "The wagon strayed a few feet off the ruts," he said to the others, shaking his head. "Suddenly it slipped into the gully. It all happened so fast!"

James looked down into the canyon again. This time he heard Will's voice rising out of it. "Sara! Sara, where are you?"

In a shot James plunged over the edge.

Two hours later all four oxen had been put down and butchered. Both wagon axles had snapped, and three of the four wheels were broken beyond repair. The wagon itself was so punched full of holes and banged up that it was good only for firewood now.

Mr. Teague offered to take Mr. and Mrs. Jennington in. The few of their possessions that hadn't been crushed in the fall were loaded onto the Teagues' wagon.

When James got to the bottom of the gully, he had found Will cradling Sara's head in his lap. He was whispering to her and stroking her hair, telling her how sorry he was. She was moaning softly.

James helped Will ease the wagon off her legs. With the aid of a few other men, who'd lowered themselves down the side of the canyon by means of a rope, they were able to carry Sara back up to the trail. By then she was unconscious.

That night the emigrants camped glumly on the banks of the placid Sweetwater.

Will sat with Sara in the Teagues' wagon, holding her hand and talking quietly to her. He'd been with her every moment since the accident had occurred.

Sara's left leg was shattered just below the hip.

There was nothing to be done. It couldn't be reset. It would have to heal itself.

When James stopped by to see how she was doing, he overheard Will saying, "I'm sorry, darling. It should've been me. I should never've let you climb into the wagon to fetch me that drink. I should've seen the danger. I should've been the one in the wagon. It should be me lying here with the busted leg. I'm sorry, I'm sorry . . ."

James knew it wasn't Will's fault. It wasn't anybody's fault.

Clearing his throat, James took a step forward. Will looked up, and beckoned him nearer.

"How are you, Sara?" James asked quietly.

"I'll live," she said feebly. Her dark hair hung limply on her shoulders, and her face looked pale and stretched. She was lying awkwardly on her right side. "The leg's giving me a twinge, but it's not so bad. What can't be cured must be endured."

James smiled wanly. She sounded like his ma.

"I wanted to thank you," Sara went on, "for helping me out of that canyon. Will told me all about it. You were truly gallant to risk yourself that way."

"Aw, it was nothing," he said. "I'd do anything for you."

"Why, that's sweet, Jamie." She bent forward to touch him, grimacing at the pain from the effort.

James wanted to climb in the wagon and hold Sara's other hand. He wanted to whisper words of comfort to her.

But he knew he couldn't console Sara, or Will. And so he bade them a sorrowful good night, leaving Sara to her pain and Will to his grief.

Six

Faces in the Ice

The sun rose blue and warm in the crisp air, but James had no heart to enjoy it. He kept to himself along the trail, not talking to anyone but Bolt. He couldn't stop thinking about Sara.

His ma was the first to notice. She was frying up supper, and James was sitting in the grass nearby, staring off into the distance. She sat down next to him. "Jamie, it's not like you to mope around so."

He shrugged.

She took his hand, but he drew it away. "Sara's a strong young woman, James. She's hurting now, it's true, but . . ."

"What can't be cured must be endured, right?"

Ma smiled. "That wasn't what I was going to say. I was going to say that she has family, and a fine young man who loves her and wants to take care of her. What more does a body need?"

James shrugged again.

"No one likes to see a loved one suffer, Jamie," Ma said kindly. "But what will help Sara most is if the people around her are strong."

James nodded. Ma leaned over and kissed him on the cheek.

"Now, you go on and round up your sister and your brother," she said. "Supper's getting cold."

Since the accident two days before, Elizabeth had stopped being so pesky around James. Whereas she'd been in the habit of shouting out questions from the wagon every five minutes—"Jamie, what kind of bird is that?" "Jamie, why are we crossing the river again?" "How much longer till we get there, Jamie?"—now she just sat staring at him with her round blue eyes.

Even Jeremy trod lightly around him, offering to do some of his chores. One time, during the midday rest, called nooning, he volunteered to water Bolt.

James appreciated his brother's efforts. But he was glad Jeremy didn't try to talk to him about what was bothering him. He didn't think he'd be able to stand it.

Cady pretty much kept her distance also, until one day she came stomping up to him at the wagon. He was shuffling along next to Bolt when she grabbed him by the shoulder and spun him around.

"I can't take it anymore, James Gregg!" she yelled.

"What're you yapping about?" he snapped back.

"You know sight well what I'm talking about, and if you don't stop it, I'm gonna . . . I'm gonna . . ."

"You're gonna what?" James laughed in her face. He knew it was mean, especially since he was aware of exactly what she was talking about. He'd been ignoring her, acting as if his worries and problems were the most important in the whole world. He'd been pitiful and selfish. But he couldn't help himself. "You're gonna *what*?" he repeated.

Cady's eyes bugged out. "I hate you, James Gregg!" she screamed. "I never want to see you again for as long as I live!" she shouted over her shoulder as she stormed off.

James stood with his mouth hanging open. He couldn't believe what he'd just done. He'd made Cady Walker, the toughest girl to hail from Philadelphia, Pennsylvania, cry.

The next afternoon James stood by the side of the trail, waiting for the Walkers' wagon to come by. He'd saddled up Bolt and was holding him by his halter. He nodded as Mr. Walker ambled past, clucking at his oxen.

Cady was tromping along behind the wagon.

"Howdy," James said, tipping his hat.

She kept her eyes locked straight ahead of her.

He fell in step beside her.

47

"I hear we're gonna be camping tonight in a field about a quarter of a mile on up the trail."

She didn't reply.

"I hear there's an ice spring nearby."

She sniffed, and stuck her nose in the air.

"I was thinking, maybe you'd like to come on over and have supper with us, and then we could explore the ice spring, you and me and Bolt. If you like, that is. Bolt here misses you." He slapped the horse's neck. "Or we could do something else if you have a better idea. Ma said you'd be welcome for supper. We're having corn cakes and fried pork. That'll be nice for a change."

Cady didn't crack a smile.

"Well, then, I guess I'll see you at supper, won't I?"

Not a peep out of her.

"Right. Well, I best be getting back to the wagon. Pa might need me for something."

James and Bolt trotted on past the Walkers' wagon. "She's a tough nut to crack," he grumbled to himself.

"That she is, boy." Mr. Walker laughed. "That she is."

Cady didn't stop by for supper that evening. When his ma asked him why she hadn't come, James pretended he didn't know.

"That poor little girl," Ma sighed, "with her sick mama and sick brother and her papa busy with the team all the time. I wish she knew she could depend on us."

James was barely able to swallow his corn cake, he felt so terrible.

After supper James led Bolt down to where he'd been told they could find the ice spring. It wasn't far. The spring was a patch of swampy ground about fifty feet across.

James knelt, and dug down through the wet dirt about six inches. Sure enough, underneath the cold soggy mud was a layer of solid greenish ice. James cleared away a patch of ice big enough to see himself in.

He looked at his reflection, all greenish and bubbly from the ice. He didn't like what he saw. He knew he'd been acting like a lout.

He'd felt worse for himself than he had for Sara. Cady's own brother was sick, possibly dying, and did she go moping around? No. In fact, Cady was braver about Scott than he'd been about Sara! He knew Sara was only being kind when she called him gallant.

He studied the face in the ice. The face of a child. The face of a coward.

"James?"

Someone else's face appeared in the ice, behind his. Cady's.

"What do you want?" he mumbled without turning around.

"I'm sorry I told you I hated you," she said. "I don't."

"Well, I'm sorry I acted the way I did." He looked up at her. "I was a no-good worthless lousy skunk. You should have slugged me."

Cady smiled. "I didn't want to get blood on my dress."

James smiled back. That was the Cady he knew. He stood up and stuck out his hand. "Forgive me?"

She grabbed it—"You're forgiven"—and shook. "Now move aside and let me see that ice spring you were so worked up about."

SEVEN

THE LITTLE SCRAP

Back and forth across the Sweetwater they wandered, crossing it a total of nine times before finally fixing on the south side. The trail began climbing the foothills of the Rocky Mountains. On either side purplish peaks hovered in the distance, some almost ten thousand feet high and still snow covered even in July.

Colonel Stewart stopped the train early one afternoon so that Pierre Delaroux would have time to lead a buffalo hunt.

The emigrants had been depending on the huge beasts almost since the first week on the trail. Every wagon had strips of buffalo meat hanging from the canopy, drying in the sun. Colonel Stewart wanted to have one last good hunt, to stock up on meat, before rolling through South Pass. On the far side of the Rockies, the buffalo would be scarce.

Pa and Jeremy were accompanying Delaroux while James stayed behind and helped Ma and Elizabeth.

"Aw, why can't I go on the hunt with you, Pa?" James asked. "I can handle a gun."

"I don't doubt you can, Jamie," Pa replied. He was saddling up Mackie. Behind him, Jeremy sat on Corncob. "But too many men on a hunt just get in one another's way. I need you back here."

Jeremy nodded in agreement, and James made a face at him.

"Now, listen here, son," Pa said sternly, mounting his horse. "Everybody has a job to do on this journey, and today yours is to help your ma. Understood?"

"Yes, sir," James said miserably. Jeremy grinned at him over their pa's shoulder.

"Good." Pa giddyapped Mackie, and he and Jeremy started off to join Delaroux. As they galloped away, Jeremy waved gleefully over his shoulder.

"Low-down sneaking whippersnapper . . ." James muttered to himself.

"James!" Ma exclaimed. She was standing right behind him. "Such talk! And about your own brother, too."

"You saw him waving at me like that, didn't you?"

"Well . . . all right, yes, I did." She ruffled his hair affectionately. "And I admit, it *was* a low-down sneaking whippersnappery thing to do. But you

52

didn't have to say so out loud." She laughed.

For some reason James didn't feel so bad about not going on the hunt. "What do you need done around here?" he asked. "Want me to water the team?"

"Oh, pshaw, Elizabeth and I can do that. You go on and do what you like. Just don't be getting yourself into any trouble."

James ran off to find Cady. She and her pa were just about done making camp. Scott was down again with a bad cough. He'd hardly been out of the wagon since the day he'd climbed Independence Rock. James sat and talked with him for a few minutes. He was so weak, he could barely speak. Mrs. Walker sat in the front of the wagon, glaring silently into the distance.

When Mr. Walker and Cady were finished, he told her she could have the rest of the afternoon off too.

A broad meadow lay not far from where the emigrants had circled the wagons for the night. Cady and James headed in that direction.

"Maybe I'll see a buffalo today after all," James said. He'd told Cady about how he hadn't been allowed on the hunt.

"Won't do us much good, since we don't have a gun," Cady observed.

"No, I expect not," James allowed. "But I like to look at 'em just the same."

They picked their way through a stand of spruce and quaking aspen. The reddish, hairy trunks of the spruce gave off a strong, pungent odor. It was like nothing James had ever smelled, but somehow it reminded him of home. He remembered walking through the cool shade of a neighbor's apple orchard, and wondered idly if he'd ever see Pennsylvania again.

The trees ended abruptly in a lush green meadow. Larkspur and blue-eyes dotted the field. Thrushes and red-winged blackbirds flitted about. Gnats floated in the yellow sunshine streaming through the tops of the trees, and fat black crickets hopped from leaf to leaf below.

"It's like something out of a storybook," Cady whispered.

"Or a dream," James added.

They stepped quietly to the center of the meadow, listening to the whistling, humming, and chirping all around them. In the far distance was a strange high burbling sound, like a chorus of babies cooing.

"It's magic," said Cady.

Then a low rhythmic beating sound, a bass-drum roll, rose out of the trees in the direction of the cooing. An immense flock of passenger pigeons came into sight over the line of treetops. The birds' fat iridescent blue bodies flashed in the sky overhead like trout darting through the clearest water.

"Look at 'em all!" James shouted, waving his hat. "Look at 'em go!"

It took many minutes for the entire flock to pass overhead.

"I reckon there were as many birds in that flock as there were buffalo in the first big herd we saw," said Cady after the last bird had disappeared over the trees. Back on the South Platte, they'd seen a herd of buffalo that went on for miles.

"At least," James agreed. He was constantly amazed at the size of the land, and the abundance of the game, in the West. "More pigeons than a man could shoot in a million years."

"Oh, they were beautiful," Cady said, "weren't they? Did you see the way their wings—" Suddenly she fell silent. "What was that?" she hissed.

"What was what?"

Then both of them heard a sound that made the hairs on the backs of their necks stand straight up.

A long, whiny howl, followed by a brief yip, came from the far side of the meadow.

The last time they'd heard a howl in the wilderness, they'd been surrounded by a pack of wolves in seconds. They'd been lucky to escape with their lives.

"Let's get out of here," James urged quietly, taking a step back. "Nice and slow. Keep calm. Don't run."

"I'm not a fool, James," Cady said under her breath. "I know better than to take off running."

"I wasn't talking to you," James whispered back angrily. "I was telling myself what to do. Now hush up."

"You're the one who was jabbering on about keeping calm!"

"Shhh!"

There was another small bark. James and Cady peered into the wood at the edge of the meadow. Something was moving in the bushes.

"James, I'm scared . . ."

"Me too . . ."

Just then a jackrabbit shot into the clearing, bounding high over the grass. Snapping at its heels, a scruffy little black-and-gray dog tore along low to the ground, yapping excitedly. The dog leaped at its intended prey, but the rabbit was quicker. It bounced sharply to one side and pranced off into the trees again.

The dog flopped down in the sunny grass, panting and whining.

"Why, it's nothing but a pup!" Cady said.

James let out a big sigh of relief. He'd seen enough wolves to last him a lifetime.

"What's a dog doing by himself way out here?" Cady said.

"Well, the Indians keep dogs," James pointed out. "Maybe it strayed away from its owner. Who knows how long it could've been wandering around?"

"Hey, poor lost fella," Cady said. She started toward the dog, which was now lying on its side with its tongue hanging out. "He looks like he's half starved to death. His ribs are sticking out."

James followed her and knelt down to scratch the dog's ears. It growled weakly, then allowed itself to be touched. Cady started petting the dog too. Soon it flopped over on its back to let its tummy be rubbed.

"I think this fella's a girl," James observed. Being a farm boy, he knew about such things. "But you were right about something else. She is starving."

He reached into his overalls pocket and drew out a corn cake.

"Why in the world are you carrying that?" Cady asked in consternation.

"A man on the trail never knows when he's gonna get hungry," James answered loftily. "Here, girl," he said softly to the dog.

He laid the cake down next to her muzzle. She sniffed it briefly and then devoured it in one quick snap.

"She *was* hungry," Cady said. "I wish we could keep her."

"Well, I reckon if she wants to follow us back to the train, we can't stop her."

They exchanged understanding smiles, then stood to go. The dog eyed them questioningly. They started walking. The dog lay in the grass, watching them leave.

When they reached the edge of the meadow, they paused and looked back. The little dog was just lying there, lost and abandoned.

"Why isn't she coming?" Cady asked.

"I don't know. Maybe she's scared."

"Maybe she needs a little encouragement."

"Hmmm. Maybe."

Then they were yelling "C'mon, girl!" and "Here, girl!" and "Good dog!" and clapping their hands, and a black-and-gray blur was racing across the grass toward them.

"But, Ma, she just followed us home," James said.

Ma frowned. "Why do I find myself doubting that's the whole truth?"

James shrugged innocently.

The little dog was lying happily in the shade of the Greggs' wagon, enjoying her third corn cake of the day.

"That's just the way it happened, Mrs. Gregg," said Cady. "Honest."

"Uh-huh," James's ma muttered.

"Please let us keep her, Ma," James repeated for the tenth time. "Please."

"Please," Elizabeth echoed. "Please!"

"I don't know, Elizabeth," Ma began. "We don't need a dog. And the trail's hard on even the strongest animals. She's scrawny as a scarecrow."

"So was Bolt when I first started caring for him," James pointed out, "and now he's healthy and strong."

"You got a point there, Jamie," Ma said, "but I still don't . . . Why, look at her!" The dog barked and wagged her tail. "She's nothing more than a little scrap."

Just then Pa and Jeremy came riding up. Each had a large slab of buffalo meat slung over the back of his horse.

"Who's the little critter?" Pa asked, pointing at the dog.

"She followed us home, Pa," James answered. He was getting tired of discussing the new dog. Why couldn't they all just let her be while she settled in? He wanted to talk about something else for a change. "Looks like you did well on the hunt."

"All right," Pa said modestly. "I shot a nice fat cow, and your brother there helped me butcher it." Jeremy concurred with a nod. Pa swung off Mackie. "Say, that little pup looks like she's half starved dead."

"Yeah, well . . ." James mumbled.

Pa drew his knife out of its sheath and sliced a long sliver of white fat off the meat strapped to Mackie. "Catch, girl," he called, tossing the fat under the wagon. The dog set on it enthusiastically.

"Land of mercy, we're stuck with her now!" Ma exclaimed, rolling her eyes to heaven.

"You don't like her, Amelia?" Pa looked as disappointed as James had a few minutes earlier.

"It's not that I don't *like* her, Sam," Ma explained. "It's just that we can't afford to be taking in every stray that comes along."

59

James noticed Cady turn a bright pink. Ma noticed it too.

"Oh, Cady dear, I didn't mean you!" She grabbed Cady and wrapped her in a big hug. "You know you're always welcome."

"Amelia, I'll admit I've been wishing for a dog," Pa said. James couldn't believe it. His pa wanted to keep her!

"She may be little, but her bark is big enough," Pa continued. "She can stand guard at night, and look after Elizabeth when we're busy. And when we get to Oregon and settle down, we'll need a good mouser. We have plenty to eat." He slapped the meat hanging on Mackie. "We'll feed her on the scraps."

"Scraps!" James repeated.

"Sure, scraps," said Pa. "You don't think she gets first pick, do you?"

"No, I meant, Scraps. That's her name. Ma said she was a little scrap, and now you said she's gonna live on scraps."

"Here, Scraps," Jeremy called. He'd reached back on Corncob and cut off a small slice of buffalo meat. Scraps darted out from under the wagon and caught the meat in the air. "She knows her name," he said, surprised.

Ma shook her head, laughing. "I see I'm outnumbered. I guess she can stay. Looks like she's going to anyway."

"Hooray!" Elizabeth shouted. "Scraps can stay."

Scraps ran around them, barking and wiggling her whole body.

James and Cady grinned at her, and then at each other. Scraps could stay. And they'd had to tell only one small fib each to make it so.

Later that evening, in the flickering light of the campfire, Scraps slept with her head in James's lap. Every now and then she gave a little kick. Probably dreaming about jackrabbits, James thought.

Jeremy sat down next to them. "Next time there's a buffalo hunt," he said, "you're welcome to go instead of me."

James was surprised. "I thought you liked hunting," he said.

"I do, when I get the chance," Jeremy said bitterly. "Pa made me stay back with the horses while he stalked the buffalo. The only reason he wanted me along was to help butcher the kill. While you were off getting yourself a new pet dog, I was up to my elbows in buffalo guts."

James couldn't help smiling to himself. He looked down at Scraps. She seemed to be smiling too. Caught that rabbit at last, he guessed.

EIGHT

SOUTH PASS

The train entered a burned-out, charred stretch of country. The trees smoldered yet from a recent fire, and the ground was still warm to the touch. A thick, acrid smoke hung in the air and blotted out the tops of the hills.

The mood of the emigrants was subdued while they rolled through the eerie, blackened landscape. Their noses and mouths were raw from breathing in smoke. When they tried to clear their throats, the spit came up an ugly brown.

Then four-year-old Jasper Smoot suddenly fell ill of cholera and died two days later. The emigrants were plunged deeper into discouragement. First Sara Gantry's injury, and now little Jasper Smoot taken away. No leaf rustled or bird sang in the wrecked, scorched stumps of trees. There was a growing feeling among the emigrants that they might never see Oregon.

James was worried about Scott in particular. His lungs were weak, and the smoke in the air could only do him harm. James found him stretched out in the back of his family's wagon. He was pale and drawn. Even lying down, he breathed heavily.

"Scott?" James whispered.

"That you, James?" came back a hoarse, feeble voice.

A lump rose in James's throat. His friend was really sick this time. "I came to see how you are."

"All right, I guess," Scott said bravely. "I thought the mountain air was supposed to be good for me," he joked. His laugh quickly turned into a gasping cough.

"We'll be clear of this burned-out land soon enough," James assured him.

"You're wrong, James Gregg," came a hissing from the front of the wagon. Mrs. Walker clambered awkwardly over a chair and trunk to hover over Scott like a witch over a cauldron. Her hair stuck out from her head every which way, and her face shone madly.

"How d'you do, Mrs. Walker," James said, trying not to meet her eye.

"It says so right here." Mrs. Walker ignored his greeting. She shook her frayed old leather-bound Bible. "'For wickedness burneth as the fire; it shall devour the briers and thorns, and shall kindle in the thickets of the forest.'" She glared down at Scott.

"You know what comes after," she prompted him.

"'And they shall mount up like the lifting up of smoke,'" Scott recited dully. He shot a pleading look at James.

Mrs. Walker smiled triumphantly. "'And they shall mount up like the lifting up of smoke,'" she repeated with satisfaction. "We'll never be clear of the fire of God's retribution, James Gregg. The Lord told me so Himself. Whispered it in my ear." She tapped the side of her head, as if to indicate which ear she was referring to.

James could feel his face flushing at Mrs. Walker's blasphemy. She claimed God had spoken to her! James knew she wasn't well, but he had no pity for her. Couldn't she see that all her talk only made Scott worse?

"I have to go now, Scott," he whispered to his friend. "I hope you start feeling better." He ran off without so much as a by-your-leave to Mrs. Walker.

The next day, despite Mrs. Walker's privileged information, the emigrants did leave the burned-out country. They began the ascent to the South Pass of the Rocky Mountains, still following the Sweetwater River.

Clean and cool in the daytime, the air was downright cold at night. Delicate crystals of white frost powdered the grass in the mornings. After the frost melted in the sun, the tangy scent of pine and fir trees filled the trail.

In the evenings, when the emigrants stoked their fires with the tough bark of artemisia, or wild sage, a greasy odor like turpentine filled the campground. At first James didn't care for it. But it represented heat, and rest, and comfort, and he soon grew fond of it. He even liked the way the artemisia flavor seeped into meat roasted over the smoky fires.

A few days before, the emigrants had been ready to roll over and give up. But now, due only to the change of scenery, their hearts were high.

Life on the trail, James observed, was like that. One day you wanted to lie down in a ditch and tell someone to shovel you under, and the next day you wanted to sing out loud with joy. Back home every day was the same. The big excitement of the year might be a cow giving birth to twins. The hardships of the journey west brought elation and despair unlike anything in Pennsylvania.

On both sides of the trail rose the jagged heights of the Rockies. Those to the north were the most impressive of all. They seemed piled one on top of another till their white summits merged into the pale horizon. James knew he would never forget the sight of those magical far-off peaks.

On July 19 the emigrants gained South Pass, a broad, gently rolling valley surrounded by mountains. Here they finally left the Sweetwater, now little more than a trickling creek, and forded several other small rivers.

. Shortly after noon Colonel Stewart ordered the wagons into the circle near a small springs at the western edge of South Pass. It was early to be making camp for the night. But since the colonel had marched the emigrants through their accustomed noon stop, they'd covered nearly the usual fifteen miles.

The colonel gathered the people on the banks of the springs. Cady and James stood side by side. Scott was back in the Walkers' wagon, with his mother.

The colonel carried a tin canteen. James wondered what he was planning to do with it.

"Folks," Colonel Stewart began, "we've had some hard times, and some good times. We've lost a few good souls—Daniel Loughery, and little Jasper Smoot. Not to mention Mr. Carver."

James shivered at the memory of the man who'd shot the Pawnee.

"But we've never lost heart," the colonel continued. "And now our journey is half over." People cheered and clapped. He motioned for quiet and held up the canteen. "This canteen is filled with water from the Sweetwater River. As you know, the Sweetwater flows to the Platte, and the Platte flows to the Missouri. The Missouri leads to the Father of Waters, the great Mississippi. And the Mississippi empties into the Atlantic Ocean."

Colonel Stewart paused dramatically and drained the canteen into the spring. "Now, these waters won't find their way to the Atlantic. They flow west, to the Big Sandy River and the Green, and eventually to the Pacific Ocean. This place is called Pacific Springs. And these are your first western waters."

The colonel ducked the canteen in the springs, raised it to his lips, and took a long draft. Then he held the canteen high over his head, wiped his long yellow mustache across the sleeve of his shirt, and smiled.

The people cheered again, and rushed forward to sample some for themselves.

James and Cady waded into the springs up to their knees. James cupped his hands under the clear cold water. He tasted it. Maybe his imagination was working too hard, but he would have sworn that the water tasted different from the eastern variety. It was colder, fresher, more satisfying.

He took another swig and looked over at Cady. She was splashing water on her face and grinning broadly at him. The water ran down her freckled cheeks. Droplets hung on her nose and chin. Sometimes, James thought, she was almost fetching. Not like Sara, of course. But a fellow could get used to her.

"What're you gaping at, mister?" she said, scooping some water at him.

"Hey!" James shouted, and splashed her back. Soon both of them were drenched from the water fight. Drenched in the waters of the Pacific.

James, despite shivering from the cold, had never been so happy to be sopping wet.

*   *   *

That night James and Cady sat together beneath a warm buffalo hide, toasting themselves in front of the campfire. James's ma had hollered at them when she saw they were wet. Didn't they know how easy it was to catch a fever?

But it had been Pa, not them, who'd taken to bed. He'd said he was feeling tuckered from the day's excitement and wanted to turn in early.

The fire crackled and hissed, and the smoke curled up into the stars overhead. Nearby, the weary oxen lowed sadly, and the horses let out an occasional snort. James could always recognize Bolt's nicker, even in the dark. Scraps had burrowed down beneath the buffalo hide and was now snoozing peacefully between James's feet.

A coyote howled in the distance. Not too long after, another one, even farther away, answered.

"James?" Cady whispered.

"Yeah?"

"What if Scott doesn't make it?"

"What do you mean?" James asked, though he knew perfectly well.

"What if Scott dies?"

James said nothing for a long moment. The silence seemed to fill up the small space of firelight they sat in, and reach into the darkness beyond.

"He'll be fine, Cady," James said at last. He knew he sounded like a liar.

"I wish I could believe that." Cady shifted, pulling

more of the hide over herself. "I'm scared, James."

Again he said nothing. It wasn't at all like Cady, who wanted everyone to think she wasn't afraid of anything, to admit she was frightened.

"My mother's expecting, you know," Cady said.

James nodded in the darkness.

"She's not well."

He nodded again, more emphatically this time.

"What'll happen to me if Scott goes and Mother can't mind the baby?" Cady asked. "Father can't care for all of us."

James felt the hide trembling, and he realized Cady was crying. Hesitantly he put his arm around her, and she buried her face in his shoulder. He hoped Elizabeth or, worse, Jeremy didn't come upon them like this.

Scraps, annoyed by the disturbance, scrambled out from under the hide. She flopped down next to the fire.

"Oh, what am I gonna do?" Cady sobbed.

James didn't know what to say. What *would* she do if Scott died and her ma couldn't care for the baby? He patted her hair softly. "There, there, it'll work out fine," he soothed. "You'll see." But he knew his words were as hollow as the feeling in his stomach.

NINE

THE DRY SANDY

"**H**and me that there line, James," said Jeremy. "And then fetch the horses and tie them to the wagon."

"Yes, sir," James grumbled, tossing his brother the leather harness strap.

James went to get the horses, which were tethered on their picket lines nearby. He didn't like taking orders from Jeremy. "Who made him boss all of a sudden?" James asked Bolt, stroking his mane. Bolt shook his head, as if he didn't know either.

When James returned, Jeremy started barking at him again: "Help Ma pack up the stove when she's done with it, and don't let Elizabeth run off."

"Soon as I tie up the horses, your majesty," James muttered.

Jeremy pretended not to hear him. "Oh, I almost forgot," he said. "Before you help Ma, make sure the kingbolt's secure. I noticed it was getting wobbly yesterday."

James ducked under the wagon. *Who made him boss?* he asked himself again. He peered up at the large bolt that connected the front axle to the underside of the wagonbed. He wasn't sure what to look for, but everything seemed all right.

"James," Jeremy called, clapping his hands. "We don't have all day. Let's go."

"I'm going, I'm going," James said under his breath, scrambling out from underneath the wagon. If Jeremy wasn't sure the kingbolt was tight enough, let him look at it himself.

The brothers were breaking camp by themselves this morning. Pa had been too weak to get up. A fever had come on him during the night, and by daybreak he was barely able to move. James and Jeremy carried him from his tent to the wagon and laid him inside.

Ma fried breakfast as she always did. She bustled around, dressing Elizabeth and preparing for another day on the trail. She chatted and clucked, and pretended all was well. But James could tell she was worried.

"Pa's going to be all right, isn't he?" James asked her when the others were out of earshot.

"Why, of course, Jamie," Ma said, brushing at a stray lock of hair that fell over her temple. "He's just feeling a little slack. What a silly question."

Her eyes smiled, but there were tears in them. James knew she wasn't telling the whole truth.

"I see," he said quietly.

Ma wiped at her eyes with the back of her hand. "Oh, Jamie, I'm sorry," she said, flustered. "I don't know what I was thinking. You're a man now, and you deserve an honest answer."

A cold feeling went all over James, like he'd been dunked in the icy waters of Pacific Springs.

"What's ailing Pa?" he managed to ask.

"I fear it's cholera, Jamie."

Cholera. The word shot through him. James knew what it meant. His pa wouldn't be able to keep down any food. And worse, soon enough he wouldn't be able to hold any water. Liquids would come right out in the form of sweat, vomit, diarrhea.

James had heard the stories: How the eyes dried out so, a man couldn't blink. How the flesh became like putty—if the skin was pinched, it didn't snap back. How the tongue swelled, how the lips cracked and split. Even with a full canteen, a man could die from lack of water in the body. It was a particularly grisly death.

Little Jasper Smoot had come down with cholera and was under the ground in two days.

"Now, Jamie, it may not be cholera," Ma interrupted his thoughts. "But if it is . . . well, your pa's a strong man. We must be strong too, and pray for him. There's always hope in the mercy of the Lord."

He knew she was right. They could only hope and pray, and make the best of it. He had to be strong for Pa, and for Ma.

"You can trust me," James began. "I know we can—"

"James!" Jeremy bellowed. "Get yourself over here and help me yoke these oxen!"

"Go now," Ma urged. "Your brother's calling you."

"Does he—?"

"I told him earlier this morning."

James ran to assist Jeremy. As he did, an unpleasant thought entered his head. The question he'd asked himself earlier that morning—who made Jeremy boss?—was answered. Evidently, Ma had.

The emigrants were entering a territory known as the Dry Sandy. The trail was flat and smooth compared to what they'd become used to in the Rockies. But the going was slow nevertheless, as the animals sank nearly six inches into the hot, loose soil with each step.

The afternoon sun hammered down out of a featureless blue sky. Water seemed to shimmer all around them, but no one tried to go swimming. The beautiful pools were nothing but mirages. The emigrants plodded forward silently, shoulders bowed, heads down.

The Dry Sandy. Whoever named it, James thought as he trudged through the ankle-deep dust, wasn't joking.

Jeremy had taken charge of driving the team. He

walked beside the animals, occasionally slapping one or the other on the hindquarters to quicken their step. It wasn't much use, however. The oxen were intent on proceeding at their own deliberate pace.

Suddenly the wagon creaked loudly, and the front end crashed down.

"Whoa, whoa!" Jeremy shouted, his voice hoarse from the dust and heat. The oxen halted immediately, thankful for the command.

James, Ma, and Elizabeth ran to the back of the wagon to see if Pa had been injured. Luckily, he'd only been startled by the fall. He hadn't been harmed.

James went around to the front of the wagon. "What happened?" he asked Jeremy.

"What does it look like?" Jeremy snapped. "The blamed front axle pulled out from under the wagon."

"Oh . . ." James got a bad feeling that he, not the front axle, was going to be blamed. "What caused it?"

"Now, how would I know?" Jeremy squatted in the dust. "It doesn't look broken. Give me a minute to figure out what went wrong."

The other emigrants couldn't stand by idly while Jeremy fixed the wagon. They had to keep moving. After assuring the Walkers that the delay was only temporary, James waved them on by. Soon the last wagon in the train rolled past.

"The kingbolt worked itself loose," Jeremy announced at long last. "That's why the wagon fell apart." He turned to James. "Didn't I ask you to look at the kingbolt this morning?"

"Uh, well, yes, you did," James allowed. "And I—"

"Can you tell me why we're stuck in the desert with a kingbolt buried in a foot of dust somewhere back there"—he waved at the trail behind them—"and no way of securing our front axle to our wagon?"

"I looked, but I didn't—"

"You looked!" Jeremy shouted, his voice cracking. "Obviously you didn't look hard enough, did you?"

"You were the one who thought the kingbolt was wobbly!" James yelled back, seething. "Why didn't you check it yourself if you know so much?"

"Boys! Boys!" Ma clapped her hands sharply. "I will not have this bickering over who's to blame. Not when your pa is ill."

James glared at Jeremy. He was angrier than a tomcat in a thunderstorm. But he wouldn't cross his ma, even to tell Jeremy what was what.

"Now, you boys are going to help me and Elizabeth look for the kingbolt," Ma said. "It can't have fallen out more than a few yards before the axle pulled away. We'll just have to search till we find it."

James and Jeremy went to work looking for the bolt. They kicked the dust from side to side, hoping to uncover it. Every now and then James accidentally booted some dust at Jeremy. One time he got him right in the face.

75

And James knew, from the way the dust kept flying at him, that Jeremy was having the same sorts of accidents.

The Greggs came straggling into the circle five hours after the rest of the train had made camp. They would have been even later if Mr. Walker hadn't ridden back to help them through the last mile or so.

After Elizabeth finally found the kingbolt, James and Jeremy had to get the axle back under the wagon and secure it properly. Another hour stalled.

Then the oxen refused to budge. They'd been resting for almost two hours and were unwilling to start up again.

Jeremy screamed at and pleaded with them, but to no avail. He cracked the whip over their heads, and they took a small step. Another crack, and another step. At last he got them moving steadily.

But their pace was even slower than it had been before. And they demanded frequent stops.

That night James was barely strong enough to unhitch the oxen and horses and water them from the canteens in the wagon. They'd been on the trail over seventeen hours that day.

And sunup was a scant six hours away.

The next day went much the same.

The sun beat down on the Dry Sandy, and the animals strained to pull through the thick dust that covered everything.

Pa was too weak to leave the wagon. He couldn't eat any solid food, and water went right through him. In a quavering voice, Ma confessed to James and Jeremy that she was convinced it was cholera.

The Greggs fell behind again. Instead of the king-bolt falling out, it was the oxen getting tangled in the yoke. The brothers couldn't cooperate in straightening the team. An hour was lost while they quarreled over who was at fault.

Once again, after the oxen rested, they refused to slog along at more than a pitifully slow rate.

Ma couldn't concern herself with helping the boys. She was busy caring for Pa and looking after Elizabeth. Will apologized for not lending a hand, but he had to look after Sara, who was still recovering from her fall.

James had taken it for granted that he could drive the team as well as his pa had. At the start of the journey, he'd even shown Mr. Walker how to crack the whip. He and Jeremy had often steered their own oxen for short stretches, and they'd done fine. But their pa had always been there to help, just in case.

Now James was learning that driving the team full-time was a different proposition. The animals insisted on setting their own pace, the way they never had with Pa. It was as if they knew James and Jeremy weren't the real bosses.

The real boss lay in the wagon, parched, feverish, barely hanging on to life.

Once again Mr. Walker had to backtrack and help the Greggs into camp. Another seventeen-hour day.

James didn't think he'd be able to force himself to rise at sunup the next morning.

Because the Greggs were on the trail late, they took the hindmost position in the train. They had to breathe the dust kicked up by everyone else. And James and Jeremy were too tired from the previous two days to drive the team properly.

Throughout the morning the Greggs fell farther and farther back, arriving at the nooning ground as the other wagons were leaving it.

James wanted to stop for an hour, even if it meant falling behind again, but Jeremy insisted they keep rolling.

"It'll be worse for us later if we don't rest now," James argued.

"We're pushing through," Jeremy said grimly. "And I don't want to hear another word about it."

James gave in, though he was sure his brother was wrong.

The afternoon sun beat down, and soon the Greggs were falling behind yet again. But at least they were coming out of the deep dust of the Dry

Sandy, and the walking was easier. Still, the oxen plodded slowly, and ahead of them the train disappeared into the distance.

James was relieved at the sight of Mr. Walker coming back to fetch them at the end of the day.

But he knew they couldn't go on like this.

TEN

THE PARTING OF THE WAYS

Early the next morning, before setting out, Colonel Stewart called the emigrants together. James dragged himself to the meeting. He was tired, and he wanted only to lie down and shut his eyes. He had no interest in whatever business the colonel wished to discuss.

Colonel Stewart paced with his hands behind his back. James was surprised to see him so agitated. Even in the face of great danger, the colonel had always seemed sure of himself. What could be bothering him?

James was aware that the train was nearing the Parting of the Ways—the famous fork in the trail where trains, friends, even families often split up, taking different routes.

The left-hand, main fork looped down to Fort Bridger, to the southwest. After making repairs and buying supplies at Fort Bridger, most emigrants headed back up in a northwesterly direction toward Oregon. A few, however, continued south and west, to the Salt Lake, where the Mormons were settling, and beyond, along the Hastings Cutoff, to California.

But not all emigrants to Oregon went by way of Fort Bridger. Some turned right at the Parting of the Ways, along Sublette's Cutoff, which led directly west toward Oregon.

After less than a hundred miles, Sublette's Cutoff rejoined the main trail in the valley of the Bear River. But because the main trail swung down to Fort Bridger, its distance to the same spot on the Bear was about a hundred and fifty miles.

Thus Sublette's Cutoff shaved over fifty miles from the trail. But James knew there were two disadvantages to the cutoff: First, because it bypassed Fort Bridger, there was no opportunity to make repairs and buy supplies. And second, the cutoff traversed rugged mountains and scorching deserts that the main trail circled around.

"Friends," Colonel Stewart began, facing the crowd, "a terrible decision has been thrust before us."

A low murmuring rose in the crowd. What "terrible decision" was upon them? James wondered. The emigrants had voted before they left Independence, Missouri, to stick to the main route through Fort Bridger rather than risk the cutoff. Why would they want to reconsider their decision?

The colonel spoke over the murmuring. "A good man, Samuel Gregg, has been laid low by cholera. I'm sure you're all aware of the difficulties his family has been having on the trail in recent days." The colonel met James's eye, then looked at Jeremy. "Despite, I might add, the valiant efforts of his two sons."

James flushed in shame. He knew they did not deserve the colonel's praise. But what did their troubles have to do with the Parting of the Ways? he wanted to ask.

"Now, John Walker has been kind enough," Colonel Stewart continued, "to ride back in the evenings to assist the Greggs. But his own family needs him, and I do not believe he can go on burning the candle at both ends."

Mr. Walker was studying the toes of his shoes as if he'd never seen anything so fascinating. Cady stood beside him, listening attentively.

"I've tried to slacken the pace these last several days," the colonel went on, "so that the Greggs would not fall too far behind. But we cannot afford to proceed in this manner."

James was shocked. He had no idea that the others had slowed on their account.

Colonel Stewart removed his hat and ran his fingers through his long yellow hair. "The question is, do we proceed apace, and leave the Greggs behind? Or do we slow down further, and possibly get caught in the western snows come fall? I leave it to you, whose fate is at stake, to decide."

The colonel walked into the crowd, which was now buzzing with debate. James had never seen him so sorrowful. It was as if he knew that however the debate went, people would get hurt.

The murmuring grew louder and louder. "We can't ask everyone to sacrifice so that one family doesn't fall back," James heard someone say.

"I don't want to leave the Greggs," another man added. "But we have to think of ourselves."

"If they can't keep up, they'll have to make do on their own," came a third voice.

James's heart was in his throat. Were they really considering leaving his family behind?

Then Will stepped up and addressed the crowd. "Fellow emigrants," he said formally. "Dear friends and companions. We're making good time." He looked from face to face. "There's no need to rush. I appeal to your better natures. Samuel Gregg is a strong man, and I'm confident he'll soon be driving—"

"It might be too late for us by then!" someone yelled.

Will ignored him. "The Greggs have won the affections of all of us. Some of us owe them our very lives. If not for the heroism of Samuel Gregg in the face of the buffalo stampede, where might we be?"

Murmurs of agreement rose from the crowd.

"Mr. Gregg has been one of our best hunters,"

Will said. "Who has not shared in the bounty of his skill?"

"Hear, hear!" someone shouted.

"Amelia is a good and gentle woman," Will observed. "Who among us has not had occasion to come to her for a kind word? Has she ever refused anyone?"

"She comforted me like an angel from heaven when my poor Daniel was drowned," the widow Loughery declared. "A finer soul you'll never find on earth."

James was amazed at how eloquently Will spoke. He seemed to be turning the crowd.

Then Eli Meacham strode forward. "We may be making good time," he said, "but we won't be for much longer if we sit around waitin' for laggards."

"No one's suggesting," Will replied, "that we sit and wait, Mr. Meach—"

"Now, I'm as fond of them Greggs as the next man," Mr. Meacham interrupted him. "Why, I gave the young'un James there a fine colt. Out of the goodness of my heart."

Liar! James almost exploded. Mr. Meacham was trying to get revenge on James in the lowest way possible.

"It breaks that same heart of mine to say it." Mr. Meacham paused, and leered at James. "But we have no choice. We gotta leave 'em behind."

"Why, you no-good, dirty—"

"Shush, James!" Will commanded. "Mr. Meacham

84

has a right to express his point of view. But I still say—"

"Remember the Donner party!" Mr. Meacham fairly screamed.

James knew that the mere mention of the Donner party shot a deep fear into every emigrant on the trail. Two winters before, the Donners had been trapped for months in the snows of the Sierra Nevadas. It was said some in the party had resorted to eating the dead to survive.

"Will you dawdle, as the Donners did, taking your time, letting the days slip on by?" Mr. Meacham asked the crowd. "Will you be stranded in the mountains when winter sets in? What will you do, without food or fuel, watching as your loved ones waste away, when you feel the pangs of a terrible hunger gnawing at your breast? What will you do then? What did the Donners do?"

The answer was too horrible to contemplate. Mr. Meacham was turning the emigrants with images of the notorious Donner party.

Will looked stricken, helpless. There were shouts of "We gotta go on!" and "Leave 'em behind!"

"I say we keep moving," Mr. Meacham concluded. "Let us not linger another day, another hour!" He glowered triumphantly at James.

James knew his family had lost.

Will took him aside. "I'm sorry, Jamie," he said. "I did my best."

"I know you did what you could, Will." In his

heart, James knew the emigrants had made the right decision. They couldn't risk themselves for the sake of one family. They had to push on.

"I'd like to stay behind with you," Will said. "You know I would. But I have responsibilities. Sara needs me. I can't leave her now. Forgive me," he pleaded. James was surprised to see tears in his eyes. "Nothing I do these days seems to be good enough. I'm failing everyone. First Sara, and now . . ."

"There's nothing to forgive," James said honestly. He wished he could say more. Instead, he grasped Will's hand and shook it. Then he went to make ready for the morning's journey.

A few minutes later, Mr. Walker came by the Greggs' wagon as James and Jeremy were yoking the oxen.

"Let me help you with that," Mr. Walker offered, taking hold of the heavy yoke James was lifting.

"No need," James grunted. "You best be heading back to your own wagon. You won't want to fall behind."

"Oh, I'm in no hurry." Mr. Walker smiled. "You see, we're sticking with you."

"*What?*" James and Jeremy said at the same time.

"You heard me." Mr. Walker squinted into the sun. "We can't abandon you now, after all you've done for us—helped us on the trail, saved Cady's life, given strength to Scott."

"But, Mr. Walker . . ." James began.

"You can't ask the whole train to risk themselves for your sakes," Mr. Walker explained, "but you can ask the Walkers. Even if you *don't* ask us, we're with you anyway. We have no choice." He laughed. "Cady insisted. And you know how hardheaded she is."

"I do know that," James agreed.

"Good." Mr. Walker nodded. "Then it's the Greggs and Walkers together, for better or worse." He turned to leave before the brothers could object further.

"Mr. Walker," Jeremy called. Mr. Walker stopped. "Thank you."

"Thank Cady, too!" James shouted after him.

That morning James and Jeremy made an effort to get along better, and so the Greggs didn't fall too far behind.

Still, it was clear that even if they worked together, they wouldn't be able to keep up for long. As Mr. Walker had promised, the Walkers dropped back with them.

Colonel Stewart halted the train at the Parting of the Ways.

"Do you think they're waiting for us?" James asked Jeremy. "I thought they'd decided not to."

Jeremy just shrugged. He was watching a man galloping toward them. Mr. Walker and Cady, and James's ma and Elizabeth, stood with the boys as the rider approached. It was Pierre Delaroux.

"Colonel Stewart and I," Delaroux addressed them, "we are filled with sorrow." He removed his beaten-up leather hat. He looked truly remorseful. "But you see, we have a responsibility to the others . . ."

"I'm sure we all understand," Ma said mildly. "It's our misfortune, and we can't ask others to share it."

Delaroux nodded. "You should know that many of your friends regretted their decision. They are not bad people. They want to help you. Madame Loughery wished to go with you. But I would not allow it. You cannot help them, I told her. You must stay with me. Er, us."

"You were right to tell her so," Ma assured him.

"So you see," he continued, "you must not blame your friends. They wanted to help you. Blame the colonel and myself if you must." He bowed humbly. "We ask your forgiveness."

"Mr. Delaroux," Ma said. "There is nothing to forgive. We understand the hardships of the trail."

Delaroux said nothing.

"Is there anything else?" Ma asked.

"One thing only," he said, brightening. "I advise you must follow the cutoff."

"The cutoff?" said Mr. Walker. "But I thought we were going by way of Fort Bridger."

"Ah, *we* still are," Delaroux replied. "And there we will make repairs and buy supplies. But if you also go to Fort Bridger, you will never catch up with us. Even if Mr. Gregg recovers, by yourselves you will fall farther and farther behind. And you may never see Oregon."

"But—" James tried to object.

"Take Sublette's Cutoff," Delaroux said. "It is shorter and faster. The ruts are clear. You will not get lost. And with luck, we will meet in the valley of the Bear. Colonel Stewart says we will reach it August 9. I hope to see you there." He turned his horse and heeled it into a gallop. "And may God speed you, my friends," he called over his shoulder as he rode away.

The Greggs and Walkers came to the Parting of the Ways. The double ruts, etched into the plain by the thousands of wagon wheels that had come before, split into two sets—one to the southwest and Fort Bridger, and one due west along Sublette's Cutoff.

Already the train was disappearing into the distance along the left-hand fork. It was the last that James, Cady, and the others might ever see of their friends.

The moment of decision had come. If they went to Fort Bridger, they could stop and rest. But the longer route would put them farther and farther behind schedule. Sublette's Cutoff was shorter, but it was also more dangerous.

Mr. Walker slowed his team. James could see the indecision in his face. Was Delaroux's advice sound?

Could the two families possibly make it by themselves through unknown territory?

The Parting of the Ways lay before them like a riddle. Which fork led to danger, and which to salvation? For many minutes no one said a word.

Then Mr. Walker shouted "Yah!" and his oxen stepped forward. They followed the ruts to the right, along the cutoff.

James would never know if Mr. Walker had chosen the route or if he had left it to fate in the form of a weary ox team.

ELEVEN

ALONG THE DANGEROUS TRAIL

After a long day of rolling across dry country, the Greggs and Walkers camped on the trail. Mr. Walker estimated they'd traveled eight miles that day. Jeremy and James went hunting jackrabbits, but neither shot one. Supper came from the wagons' store of jerked beef and johnnycakes. Water out of a canteen.

A few miles to the west, a rounded butte shaped like a haystack broke the featureless sagebrush plain. Delaroux had been correct about the ruts—they were clear and deep. It was impossible to get lost. So far, at least.

Everyone but Mrs. Walker and James's pa gathered around the sagebrush fire that night.

James's pa was too weak to leave the wagon. Ma was cheered that he wasn't getting worse—the fever was down, and he was able to hold some water. She was convinced he'd live. But he still couldn't keep solid food in his stomach, and he'd lost a lot of weight. Even if he recovered soon, it would be weeks before he had all his strength back.

Mrs. Walker refused to leave her wagon for anything. She was fat around the middle from the baby growing inside her, but otherwise, James thought, she was as gaunt and drawn as Pa was.

Cady and James sat under the buffalo hide. James hoped she wouldn't want him to hold her, the way she had that other night. It was embarrassing.

Cady plucked at the thick woolly fur of the hide. "You and Jeremy haven't been getting along well lately," she commented.

"No, I reckon not," James said.

She stared into the fire. "We're going to need you both if we want to make it to the Bear River alive."

James wondered what she was driving at. "I don't know about Jeremy, but you can count on me," he said tersely.

"Father was hoping you'd put away your differences," she said. "I was too."

"We wouldn't have differences if he'd stay out of my way," James said hotly. Across the fire, Scott looked up at them. Then quietly, so no one but Cady could hear, James added: "He thinks he can order me around."

"He *is* your older brother, James," she observed.

"But he's not my pa," he argued. "Sometimes I almost wish he had run back to Pennsylvania when he'd had the chance. Now let's drop it, all right?"

"All right." Cady tossed a stone into the fire. "Just remember, the day may come again when you're glad to have him."

They passed Haystack Butte, then crossed Sublette's Flat, a perfectly level stretch of land about three miles across. Here the shallow ruts divided into numerous sets—evidence of where, in years past, trains had broken formation, the wagons racing across the hard earth a dozen abreast.

James's spirits rose as they crossed the flats. Though the day was hot, and there was no food or game in sight, this stretch of road was the easiest of the trip. The ground was smoother than the tended streets of Independence, Missouri.

If all of Sublette's Cutoff was so simple, James thought, they'd beat the main train to the Bear River with days to spare.

He hoped it would be so.

But soon they came upon a steep, rocky canyon. It stretched off for miles in either direction. There was no choice but to descend hundreds of feet down treacherous, unsteady trails, then fight back up the opposite side.

The ruts wove in and out of each other, as if the emigrants who had come before had never figured out the one best way to get up and down the canyon.

93

The wagons hugged the edges of sharp cliffs, wound around huge boulders and outcroppings of jagged rock, and plunged down gravelly inclines that abutted steep grades.

Here and there along the trail were the bleached skeletons of oxen, cattle, and horses. Names carved into rocks marked the places where people, too, had perished.

At the bottom of the canyon was a small stream. The Walkers and Greggs filled their canteens and watered their animals. James had noticed that his family's two oxen were looking particularly weary. The horses—Mackie, Corncob, and Bolt—had sore hooves, but in general were healthy. Scraps was spending most of the days in the wagon with Pa, who was happy for the company of the little dog.

The Walkers' four oxen, now that the wagon was lighter, were holding up better. James wasn't sure how much farther his family's team could go.

Sublette's Cutoff was earning its daunting reputation.

When they made it out of the first canyon, they had to descend another one equally steep. The days went by in a blur, each filled with struggle, dust, and diminishing hope.

Pa had recovered from the cholera, but he was far too weak to walk or help drive the team. James and Jeremy spoke only when absolutely necessary. James knew they were behaving poorly, but until his pa was well enough to take charge of the wagon again, he refused to take orders from Jeremy. And Jeremy insisted on acting like he was boss.

Out of the second canyon, and into the third. At the bottom of it, Mr. Walker said, lay the Green River.

The canyon of the Green was the most treacherous yet. The trail was so narrow in places that the teams had to be unhitched so the oxen could proceed single file. Repeatedly the wagons were unloaded and their contents lowered by ropes ten, fifteen, even twenty feet. Then the wagons themselves were let down.

In these places, those who couldn't walk—Pa, Mrs. Walker, Scott—had to be lowered by rope as well. Scott was so frail, James estimated he weighed no more than seventy-five pounds. But Pa and Mrs. Walker were heavier. James didn't know how he, Ma, Cady, Jeremy, and Mr. Walker were able to do it, but they got everyone down safe.

The bottom of the canyon was littered with the rotting fragments of smashed wagons—all that was left of the dreams of countless unfortunates who'd come before.

They made camp on the banks of the Green, where there was a small settlement of Mormons who operated a ferry across the rough water.

The next morning the Mormons, for a fee of two dollars a wagon, rafted them across the Green. The date was July 25. They had fifteen days to reach the valley of the Bear.

All that day and into the next they struggled up the canyon of the Green. The trail was confusing, as the ruts split apart and merged and wandered off into spurs that led nowhere. James wished they had with them Colonel Stewart or Pierre Delaroux or someone else who knew the country and could tell them which road to follow.

But as Delaroux had promised, they had not gotten lost, at least not for long. When in doubt, they followed the sun west, and always met up with some ruts. But they surely could have saved time spent pursuing fruitless paths and circuitous routes.

The days were unrelentingly hot. After leaving the Green, they found no fresh water for miles. James wondered how the emigrants in the main train were doing. Probably they were enjoying the comforts of Fort Bridger now.

One evening James and Jeremy decided to go out hunting. The families hadn't had fresh game in weeks. Even roast gopher would be a welcome improvement over another night of dry jerky.

Cady wanted to try her hand at hunting, but James wouldn't let her.

"You've never fired a gun," he said.

"It doesn't look that hard." She stuck out her jaw. "Just point and pull the trigger."

James rolled his eyes. "There's more to it than that. You have to know how to load it. There's powder, lead, caps. You have to cock it properly. And you have do it without shooting yourself in the foot."

"You could show me," Cady suggested.

"Maybe I will," James replied. "When we have the time."

James wanted to follow a small gully and go after rabbits or other small game in the brush. But Jeremy preferred sticking to higher ground.

"We'll get a better shot at antelope on the flats," he said.

"Not if they see us coming," James muttered. But he did as his brother insisted. He knew there was no point in arguing.

The two brothers hiked two or three miles across the plain without seeing so much as a field mouse.

Then suddenly a buffalo came ambling around a low butte, followed by two others. James couldn't believe it. They were the first buffalo he'd seen since crossing South Pass.

"You stay here," Jeremy whispered. "I'll sneak around the ridge." He pointed to a hillock in the west.

"No," James said. "The wind's coming from over there. You'll spook 'em. We should circle around that way"—he motioned away from the ridge Jeremy had indicated—"and fire at 'em from the east."

"They'll see us coming from over there!" Jeremy hissed. "Now do as I say. Stay here and watch me bag us some supper."

Without another word Jeremy scuttled off toward

the ridge. James lay low, as he'd been told.

Sure enough, before Jeremy could get off even a single shot, the buffaloes snorted and bucked, and started trotting off.

"Tarnation . . ." James muttered to himself, springing to his feet. He ran after the buffalo, hurriedly loading his rifle. The small herd broke into a gallop when they saw him.

James fired after them, and then Jeremy, who'd also come running, got off a shot. But it was in vain. The buffaloes were too far away.

"Why'd you go chasing after 'em?" Jeremy screamed. "Didn't you see I was ready to shoot?"

"I saw buffalo hightailing it away from us!" James yelled back. "They smelled you just like I said they would!"

The brothers kept shouting for another fifteen minutes, blaming each other for the day's lost meal. Finally they grew tired of hollering and trudged toward camp in silence, each hating the other.

As they neared the wagons, however, they put aside their disagreement.

Pa was not in the wagon. He was stretched across the ground. A man stood over him, while another man held Ma by the arm. The two men were carrying rifles, and they had them pointed at their prisoners.

James and Jeremy dove behind a tangle of sage to avoid being spotted.

"Desperadoes!" James whispered.

TWELVE

REUNION

"They've got Pa and Ma," Jeremy said quietly. "And look."

James poked his head out from around the sagebrush. He saw a third man aiming a rifle at Cady and Mr. Walker. Mr. Walker's gun lay on the ground beside him.

"We have to save them!" said James.

"It's not going to be easy," Jeremy shot back.

"This whole blame trip hasn't been easy," James muttered testily, "but we have to do it anyway." He thought for a moment, squinting his eyes at the scene before him. His heart was thudding heavily in his chest.

James's ma was holding Elizabeth tightly on her lap. Elizabeth was crying. James felt Jeremy tense beside him when one of the men seemed to speak harshly to her. Ma pulled her closer, and

Elizabeth buried her face in Ma's shoulder.

"We need some kind of plan," Jeremy said under his breath.

Well, of course we do, James thought. It irked him that Jeremy was trying to take charge of this, too. On the other hand, he knew he would have to work with his brother to save his family. He turned his mind to figuring out a rescue plan.

"Are you sure there are only three?" he asked quietly.

"Only?" Jeremy replied.

"Well . . . why can't we just take 'em?" James wondered aloud. "We have rifles."

He pictured himself storming up to the wagon, the desperadoes surprised, terrified. He raised his gun and . . . and what? He had never shot a man before. Never even shot *at* one.

"Nope, don't think so," Jeremy said. "They got a gun on Ma. Besides, there's three of them, and only two of us." He was very quiet and still.

One of the desperadoes commenced dragging the supplies out of the Greggs' wagon, flinging them onto the ground. He snatched at a long strip of dried meat hanging from a rafter and began gnawing on it.

"They must be hungry," Jeremy observed. "That one's eating dried buffalo, straight."

Dried meat was as hard and stiff as shoe leather, and about as easy to eat. James's ma always soaked it in boiling water or stewed it for a long time before anyone could get their teeth through. The desperadoes must not have eaten for days.

"How 'bout we come around on them from two sides," James suggested. "Like with the buffaloes."

"Oh, *that* worked well," Jeremy snapped. "Now hush up and let me think."

James had to bite his lip to keep from jumping up and whacking Jeremy with the butt of his rifle. He looked again toward the wagon. Cady, sitting near James's pa, was peering around, as if searching for someone. James waved his hat slightly at her, and she caught sight of it. He smiled to himself as she coolly looked in another direction. She was smart enough not to give them away.

Then James saw Pa raising his hand weakly. Ma reached out to give him water, but the desperado slapped down her hand.

Suddenly Scraps dashed out from under the wagon and clamped her teeth around the desperado's boot. But she was so small, the desperado simply kicked out, sending her flying against the wagon. Before she could rush at him again, the man kicked her hard in the side. Scraps lay in the dust, stunned.

The images blurred from the tears in James's eyes. He had never been so furious in his life. He wanted to kill that man, skin him like a buffalo, leave his corpse for the buzzards and ants.

"Can you make a sound like a prairie chicken?" Jeremy whispered. "I have a plan."

*   *   *

"*Crck crck crck crr-aawk!*" James made a noise halfway between a cluck and a crow.

This was the stupidest plan he'd ever heard. Why had he let Jeremy talk him into it?

He wasn't sure he sounded much like a prairie chicken. He knew he sounded ridiculous. And he didn't think prairie chickens even lived in this part of the country. But no matter. If he sounded anything like supper to the desperadoes, this crazy plan might work.

He was hiding behind a low outcropping of rock, a hundred yards away from the wagons. Above him, on top of a boulder, lay Jeremy. He was holding his loaded but uncocked rifle by the barrel end, ready to swing the butt down. James hoped his brother wouldn't have to fire the gun. And if the gun did fire, James hoped it wasn't when Jeremy, holding the barrel, swung it!

Jeremy's original idea had been to lure one of the desperadoes away by imitating a chicken, then shoot him. That would even the odds. Two against two.

But James had pointed out that the shot would alert the other desperadoes. At first they might think that it was just their companion shooting at the chicken. But if he didn't return with the catch right away, they'd grow suspicious. They might harm their prisoners, even shoot them in revenge.

By striking with the rifle butt, James argued, the

first desperado could be taken out silently. Then the brothers would have time to plan their attack on the other desperadoes.

Jeremy had agreed to do it James's way.

"Crr-aawk crck crck!" James called as loudly as he could. He huddled behind the rock, thinking Jeremy'd better hit the desperado before he got off a shot at the "prairie chicken." They'd get only one chance.

James was about to let out another crow when Jeremy pressed his finger to his lips. James could hear footsteps on the far side of the rock. His heart thudded in his ears, and he felt a sweat break out all over his body. He might be killed in the next few seconds if Jeremy didn't—

Thwack! Jeremy's rifle butt connected squarely with the crown of the desperado's grimy leather hat. The man issued a small grunt, pitched forward, and crumpled onto the ground.

James scrambled over and grabbed the man's rifle. He pointed it at the desperado's head. His hands were trembling so much, he took his finger off the trigger for fear of pulling it accidentally.

The desperado lay as still as death.

"You reckon you killed him?" James whispered.

Jeremy hopped down from the rock. He looked at the man consideringly. "I doubt it," he decided.

With a coil of rope he'd been carrying to string up any game they might catch, he bound the man's hands and feet. He worked quickly and calmly, yanking the knots tight. Then he jammed his hand-kerchief into the man's mouth. "That oughta keep him. For a while, at least."

"What do we do now?" James asked.

Jeremy shot him a look of mock astonishment. "My little brother, asking my opinion?"

"Well, the chicken plan worked," James admitted.

Jeremy looked pleased. "It wouldn't have worked as well without your suggestion," he said graciously.

The two brothers looked at each other for a long moment.

"And . . . so?" said James.

"And so what?"

"So I thought maybe you had an idea for the other two."

"Ummm . . . no. Not yet. I'm still working on it."

James reflected for a minute. "It's two against two now, just like you wanted."

"Yeah?"

"You aim for one and I'll aim for the other." James shrugged. "If we both hit our marks, it'll all be over."

"And if one of us misses?" Jeremy sneered. "It might be over for Ma. Or Pa. Or Elizabeth. Not to mention one of the Walkers."

"What do you suggest we do, then?" James asked angrily. "Repeat the prairie-chicken trick two more times?"

A thoughtful look came over Jeremy's face.

"You can't be serious," James wailed.

"Start clucking," Jeremy replied, climbing back up the boulder.

The three desperadoes, bound hand and foot, lay side by side like sacks of potatoes. Mr. Walker stood over them, shaking his head.

"And you say you just hid behind the rock, then hit them over the head with your rifle?" he asked James and Jeremy for the fifth time.

The brothers nodded. Ma moved from one to the other, hugging and kissing them, telling them how clever and brave they were. Elizabeth skipped about, shouting excitedly. Scraps, limping a little from the desperado's blow, barked and pranced happily.

"Why don't you tell everyone the *whole* story, James?" said Cady, teasing. "I was keeping lookout for you in camp. Jeremy was whacking the desperadoes with the rifle. But what were *you* doing?" Her eyes danced mischievously. "Now, I do recall hearing some squawking that sounded like a sick buzzard. You know anything about that?"

James glanced away. "Must've been your imagination." He and Jeremy had decided that the trick would be their secret.

"In any case," said Mr. Walker, "you boys did good work. These are dangerous men. They live like animals, in caves, coming out to steal horses and oxen to trade to Indians. Oftentimes they kill their victims. You boys probably saved all our lives."

"Glad to be of help, sir," said Jeremy modestly. "But now what do we do with these fellows?"

The desperadoes were just coming to. They were moaning softly and writhing on the ground a little.

"We can't just leave them here." Mr. Walker scratched his forehead. "I reckon we should loosen the ropes on their feet, so they can walk. But we should keep them hobbled, so they can't run, and tie them together in a chain."

"You think they'll keep up with us, tied together?" James asked.

Mr. Walker shrugged. "If they can't, we leave them to die in the sun. We can't slow the pace for their sake."

James nodded in agreement.

"We'll have to keep a gun on them at all times," Mr. Walker continued. "Jeremy, will your pa be up to that during the day?"

"I expect so," Jeremy replied. "If he can do it from the wagon."

"Good. I'll arrange it," said Mr. Walker. "We'll have to take shifts watching them at night. And again, if it gets to be too much of a strain, we leave them behind. If they're lucky, we'll hand them over to Colonel Stewart at the Bear. And what *he* does with them is none of our concern."

James thought Mr. Walker's plan was a good one.

He met his brother's eye. They'd acted together in catching the desperadoes—even if the act had been a bit humiliating. James couldn't help wishing they'd come out, rifles blazing, and made the rescue in more spectacular fashion. But they'd done their best. And it was good enough.

Six days later, after crossing numberless dusty canyons and sandy flats, the Greggs and Walkers finally crested the ridge overlooking the Bear River.

James let out a whoop when he saw, down in the valley, about five miles distant, the white canvas covers of the Stewart train.

Though they were weary fit to drop, the Greggs and Walkers dashed down the slope, hollering and hallooing all the way. Behind them straggled the three desperadoes, hands still tied behind their backs, their ankles still roped together.

In the week since they'd been captured, the three desperadoes had uttered barely a word among them. They wouldn't say who they were, where their horses were hid, or if there were more to the gang.

Several times they'd tried to sneak off, but they'd never got far. A rifle shot just over their heads always convinced them to come back.

Still, their sullen silence had made James uneasy. But now Colonel Stewart would take charge of them. James was confident a military man would have no problem dealing with prisoners.

107

Will was first to meet the families as they rolled down the slope. "I knew you'd make it!" he shouted, grappling first James, then Jeremy, around the shoulders. Then he spotted the three bound men stumbling along behind. "Who're those fellows?"

"Oh," Jeremy said offhandedly, "just some desperadoes. James and I captured them last week."

Colonel Stewart and Pierre Delaroux rode up on their horses.

"Welcome back, my friends," Delaroux said, grinning. "Sublette's Cutoff, it is a good trail, no?"

"No, it is *not* a good trail," Mr. Walker replied. "I never wish to see it again." He smiled broadly. "But thanks to your good advice, Mr. Delaroux, we're here on schedule."

Delaroux tipped his hat and laughed loudly.

Then the colonel spoke up. "I believe I know these fellows," he said. He was looking at the three desperadoes. "You there," he addressed the tallest one. "Aren't you Tom Clampson?"

Clampson! James recognized the name. It was the name of the fellow he'd seen hanged at Fort Laramie. And Tom Clampson had killed a man in a saloon back in Independence, Missouri.

Tom Clampson spat on the ground in reply to the colonel's question.

"And you," Colonel Stewart said to the second desperado. "You're Ben Clampson." He moved to the third man. "And you're Doc Pritchett."

Doc Pritchett sneered silently.

The colonel smiled at the Walkers and Greggs. "These here are the Clampson boys, three of the most wanted men in the West," he said. "The authorities at Fort Hall will be mighty glad to see them. How on earth did you catch them?"

Mr. Walker turned to James and Jeremy. "Care to tell the story—the *real* story—boys?"

THIRTEEN

ALONZO TANNER

That night the emigrants circled up the wagons on the banks of the Bear. The Greggs took their accustomed place behind the widow Loughery and ahead of the Walkers.

James felt safe for the first time in weeks. "It's like coming home," he said to Cady.

"More like your home than mine," she replied. "No one could take the Bear River for Philadelphia. But still, I'm glad to be here."

Mr. Smoot got out his fiddle, and Mr. Moss joined him on the concertina. When Harlan Teague started calling out a square dance, the party really began. Everyone was happy for the return of the Greggs and Walkers. Everyone but Mr. Meacham, that is. He eyed James darkly, then disappeared into his wagon.

James danced several energetic rounds with his ma. When Pierre Delaroux, who was surprisingly light on his feet, wasn't spinning her around, James danced with the widow Loughery.

Cady kept trying to catch his eye as he swung past, but he kept glancing away quickly. Finally he gave in and asked her to dance.

Unfortunately, just at that moment Mr. Smoot and Mr. Teague broke into a sad, slow air.

James realized he would have to slow-dance with Cady. He clasped his left hand to her right. He put his other hand on the small of her back, trying to keep a safe distance between them. Cady laid her head on his shoulder, shut her eyes, and sighed. He turned a bright crimson.

Beyond her James saw Will and Sara moving outside the circle of dancers. It was the first time he'd seen Sara walking since the accident. She limped badly, bracing herself on Will's shoulder. One hip appeared to be higher than the other. She winced with each step.

When Sara noticed him looking her way, she smiled brightly and waved. At the same time, Will winked and nodded approvingly. Cady was clasping James like she never intended to let go. He blushed even more deeply.

The dances went on and on. James took more turns with his ma and the widow, sat out a couple to visit with Will and Sara, and even danced with Cady again. He made sure it was a quick reel the second time, though.

Night came on, and the emigrants gathered around a large bonfire of cottonwood branches. Sparks sailed up into the black sky, glowed dimmer and dimmer, and merged with the silvery stars. The revelers were weary from the journey, yet they didn't retire. First they wanted to hear some tales.

"I'd like to raise a cheer," Will began, "in honor of two fine young men, who not only saved their own family, but saved the Walkers as well. The bravest pair of trailblazers ever to set foot in the West—Jeremy and James Gregg."

Everyone shouted "Hurrah!" James had never felt so embarrassed, nor so pleased, in all his life. By the big silly grin on Jeremy's face, he could tell his brother felt the same.

After the cheer died, Colonel Stewart spoke. "Now, the Gregg boys certainly are worthy of our admiration and respect." He puffed on his long-stem pipe and blew the smoke toward the sky. "And rounding up three desperadoes is a right good trick. But the bravest ever to set foot in the West?"

"That's right," Will asserted. "You know any braver?"

The colonel squinted into the firelight. "Ever hear of a mountain man name of Alonzo Tanner?"

"Can't say as I have, Colonel," Will returned.

"A braver heart than Alonzo Tanner's never beat in human breast," the colonel declared, looking around at the circle of listeners. No one dared contradict him.

"He was brave as a lion," the colonel said. "Brave as a bear. In fact, one summer—this was before I met him—Alonzo Tanner was set upon by a bear. All alone in the woods he was, with nary gun nor knife. Just his bare hands, and the bear snapping its teeth and waving its claws and coming for him."

"I'd've run for the hills," James whispered to Cady.

Colonel Stewart overheard him. "Well, now, Mr. Gregg, that's just what I'd have done too." He sucked on his pipe. "But not Alonzo Tanner. He was braver than you or I. He grabbed that bear around the middle and wrestled him to the ground. They rolled around something awful, the bear hallooing and scratching and biting, and Alonzo Tanner hanging on for dear life. Over and over they rolled, from one end of the forest to another, up hills and down valleys, over bushes and through brambles, till finally they slid onto a frozen pond—"

"I thought you said it was summertime!" Will piped up. The crowd hooted in agreement.

"Indeed it was, when they started," said the colonel mildly. "By now it was December. Any other man would have given up in October. But not Alonzo Tanner. He'd've wrestled that bear till February.

"But when they got on the ice, Alonzo Tanner knew he wouldn't have to. He stood up, and when the bear went to stand, his paws slipped out from under him. Alonzo Tanner quick as a flash reached down inside that bear's mouth, grabbed him by the tail, and pulled him inside out. And that was the end of the bear."

The crowd laughed appreciatively at the colonel's tale.

"Sounds like Alonzo Tanner was better at telling stories than he was at fighting bears," Will joked. The others around the fire guffawed loudly. "If this was before you met him, how do you know it's true?"

"Why, I saw the bear," the colonel replied. "At night Alonzo Tanner crawled into the mouth of that old inside-out bear and slept like a baby. Claimed it was cozier than a featherbed."

"He got you there!" someone shouted at Will as the others crowed in approval at the colonel's quick reply.

"That may be," Will allowed. "But I'm still not convinced Alonzo Tanner was braver than my friends Jeremy and James. You'll have to do better than an inside-out bear, Colonel. Why, I bet your Alonzo Tanner would've run at the first sight of the desperadoes my boys brought in."

The colonel looked thoughtfully at the fire for a long moment. Then he said, "Alonzo Tanner's bravery was tested time and again, my friend. Once, in the Mexican War, we fired him on a cannonball over Palo Alto. Everyone knew it was a suicide mission.

But after spying on the enemy, he hopped on a cannonball going the other direction and came back safe and sound. Then there were the times he whipped three panthers in a fair fight and stopped four bandits with a single shot.

"But I'm going to tell you of Alonzo Tanner's greatest act of bravery. And it didn't have to do with war, or beasts, or shooting even a single man. You say Alonzo Tanner would have run from the desperadoes. Well, sometimes running is the bravest course of all, as you'll shortly see."

The colonel's voice dropped to near a whisper. "Alonzo Tanner and I were packing through the Bitterroots, taking some beaver pelts up to Thompson's old trading post. This must have been, oh, well nigh eighteen years ago.

"I was a young buck then, full of spunk, always ready with a flattering word to the ladies. I had me a sweetheart in Albany—my own dear Dorothy, who later became my wife, God rest her."

Colonel Stewart paused, staring thoughtfully at the fire. James hadn't known he was a widower—it was hard to imagine a man like the colonel with any kind of family.

"But Alonzo Tanner, he was a mountain man. His only love was the out-of-doors. He may have been brave, but he was as wild and shaggy as the bear he slept in. He had no time for womenfolk. And besides, who would want a man like him?"

James couldn't imagine any girl would.

"So we were up in the Bitterroots, as I say. In a pretty green valley we come upon an Indian village. We go up to the chief's house, and here's a young maid sitting out front."

Colonel Stewart took a long drag on his pipe. "Alonzo Tanner is struck dumb at the sight of her. It's love at first sight for him.

"Now, it happens she was the chief's daughter, name of Pocalalla. And despite Alonzo Tanner's grizzly face and rough clothes, Pocalalla falls in love with him too, right there on the spot.

"Unfortunately, the chief has promised her to the son of a neighboring chief. When Alonzo Tanner asks for the maid's hand, the chief turns him down flat. What does Alonzo Tanner, a wild mountain man with nothing more than the pelts slung over his shoulder, have to offer the daughter of an important chief?"

The colonel paused. James reckoned he must have something.

"Nothing. Nothing at all," said the colonel. "So the chief orders his daughter, now all crying and tearing her hair out over the loss of her own true love, into the house. And he sends Alonzo Tanner packing. He threatens to kill both him and Pocalalla if he steps foot in the village again. And the chief has thirty braves to back him up on the threat, too.

"So that's that, thinks I. Even Alonzo Tanner, who

whipped three panthers in a fair fight, can't defeat ten times as many braves.

"We start out on the trail, but we haven't gone a hundred yards when Alonzo Tanner stops. Pocalalla is wailing in the distance. Alonzo Tanner can't take another step or his heart will break. But he can't go back to the village, either.

"He's a brave man and would gladly die for love, of course. But the last thing he wants is to kill the maid by entering the village. He can't go forward, and he can't turn back. So what do you suppose he does?"

The colonel eyed the crowd. No one, not even Will, had an answer.

"Alonzo Tanner starts running around the village, neither coming closer in nor going farther away. He runs and runs, fifty times around that village. He's hoping to knock the love for Pocalalla right out of himself, so he can leave the village in peace.

"He's sprinting like a jackrabbit, loping like a coyote, galloping like a buffalo, crashing through the brush, tearing up the earth. I knew then that he wasn't wrestling a mere bear. He was wrestling his own heart.

"Night falls, and Alonzo Tanner's still running and the maid's still wailing. The sun comes up. A hundred times now around the village and Alonzo Tanner's still running. Two hundred, five hundred, seven hundred times he circles the village. The days go by, and Pocalalla's crying like her body's been torn in half.

117

"Now, this was a man who'd wrestled a bear for six months. He's never going to run himself out. Finally he knows he can't win. So after the thousandth time around the village, he turns and starts right for it. Thirty braves have their bows drawn, and he's walking toward them calm as you please. I was sure I'd witnessed the last mortal hour of old Alonzo Tanner.

"But the chief never gives the order to fire. Seems he'd rather break his word to the neighboring chief than slay a man like Alonzo Tanner, whose bravery was bested only by his love."

The colonel sucked on his pipe. "Alonzo Tanner went to the chief's house, took Pocalalla in his arms, and carried her away." He knocked his pipe on the ground and kicked out the embers. "And that's how running was the bravest thing Alonzo Tanner ever did," he concluded.

"Why, Colonel Stewart," Sara said. "That's about the most romantic tale I ever did hear."

James thought it was mushy. He liked the bear story more.

"And every word of it's true," the colonel said to Sara and Will. "Now I'll bid you all good night." He stood up, stretched, and strode out of the firelight.

"Just think," Cady said dreamily. "Alonzo Tanner loved Pocalalla so much, he ran around the village a thousand times."

"That's not so many," Jeremy said. "I'd've done twice that many for Missy."

"How did the colonel put it?" Cady ignored him. "A man 'whose bravery was bested only by his love.'" She sighed long and loud. Jeremy sighed with her.

James snickered silently at Cady and at his brother. Didn't they know the colonel had made the whole thing up?

But before James fell asleep that night, he pondered the tale of Alonzo Tanner. Though he knew it wasn't really true, he couldn't help suspecting there was truth in it somewhere.

FOURTEEN

THE LITTLE HERO

Left, right, left, right. James put one foot in front of the other. Step, step, step. He walked along. Walk, walk, walk, mile after unchanging mile.

James had noticed how life in the train swung from happiness to sorrow and back again much faster than it did back home. There was danger, villainy, heroism. Each day was a new adventure. In that respect, the trail was more interesting than the farm outside Franklin had been.

But he also noticed that individual hours were far more boring than any hour back home had ever been. In Pennsylvania, he could swim or climb a tree or catch a squirrel when he was bored. Here all he could do was keep walking. Walk, walk, walk. Left, right, left, right. Step, step, step.

Even school was less boring than this.

120

The Bear River valley was beautiful, he had to admit. Alders and dogwood shaded the trail. Hawthorn bushes grew in clumps, their sweet berries ripe for the picking. Black-tailed deer and elk moved silently among the tree trunks. The river itself was full of speckled trout nearly two feet long. Ducks, geese, and herons waded among the milkweed on the banks.

But James marched on past it. Left, right, left. One foot in front of the other. One step after another. One step closer to Oregon.

He wondered if Scott would ever be strong again. If not, and if his ma didn't recover either, what would become of Cady? And would Will ever stop blaming himself for Sara's accident? He was wrong to, James knew. But how could James convince him of it?

Then he thought about Jeremy. Would his brother stay with the family when they got to Oregon? The call of gold in California was powerful. Other emigrants had heard it too. There was talk some might head south when the train reached the California Trail fork.

James was idly turning over these thoughts when Cady skipped up beside him.

"We'll be nooning in another hour," she said.

"I can't wait." James kicked a stone down the rut he was following. "I am so tired of walking."

"You're not about to break down like an old plow horse, are you, James?" Cady teased. She picked up the stone James had kicked and tossed it into the woods. "Me, I got all the energy in the world."

"I'm not tired weary," James said. "I'm tired bored. It seems like I've been walking every day of my whole life."

"Oh, it hasn't been *that* long," she assured him. "And anyway, we'll be in Oregon City before you know it. Then you'll miss the days on the trail, not to mention your good friend Cady Walker."

James gave her a playful shove. "I may miss the trail someday, but I'm sure I'll never miss *you*."

She smiled and shoved him back. "I know you're just saying that, James, 'cause you're shy. All you farm boys are. It's something we sophisticated city ladies have to put up with."

James laughed, and commenced kicking another stone down his rut. Cady jumped into the other rut and kicked at a stone.

For the next hour, until nooning, they played at who could kick a stone farthest and not have it pop out of the rut. James was not surprised that Cady was as good at it as he was.

During nooning James's ma wanted time alone to devote to chores. So she asked James and Cady to look after Elizabeth.

"Take Scraps with you too," she said. "Every time I turn around, that dog is trying to climb into the wagon."

"She likes Pa," James pointed out. Though Pa

was recovering, he was too weak to walk more than two or three hours a day. He still spent most of his time in the wagon.

"*I* think she likes buffalo meat. I don't know why I tolerate that pesky dog . . ." Ma gave James a crinkly-eyed smile. "Or any of you, for that matter. Now run along and let me have some peace."

James took Elizabeth by the hand. "Here, girl," he called to his dog. Scraps came sprinting out from under the wagon, yapping happily.

Elizabeth giggled, and tossed a stick. Scraps darted after it and pounced. She had never been taught to fetch, so she didn't know that Elizabeth wanted her to return the stick. Instead she growled over it fiercely, which set Elizabeth to giggling even harder.

"Scraps sure is a funny dog, James," Cady said.

"She's brave, too," he added.

"Not as brave as Alonzo Tanner."

"Maybe not. But plenty brave for a little dog." James tossed another stick, and Scraps ran after it. "Remember how she tried to bite that desperado?"

"That was brave," Cady allowed. "But it didn't do much good. He just kicked her aside."

"That doesn't mean anything," James argued. "The point was, she *tried.* Just like Alonzo Tanner." James had spent considerable time pondering what made Alonzo Tanner brave. "The colonel said the brave part was when Alonzo was running around the village—not when he faced the thirty

123

braves. Why do you suppose he said that?"

James waited for Cady to answer. "I'm not sure," she said.

"It was 'cause facing the braves was selfish," he explained. "Alonzo was putting Pocalalla in danger. But running around the village was like Scraps biting the desperado. Both of them knew they couldn't win, but they did it anyway. *That's* bravery."

"I didn't look at it like that," Cady admitted. "I just liked the idea of him loving the maid so much."

James sighed. That was the very part of the story he *hadn't* liked.

"I liked it when he slept in the bear," Elizabeth volunteered. "That was funny."

"That *was* funny," James agreed, ruffling his little sister's hair. They were on the bank of the river. "You go on down, but don't play in the water. I don't want to have to fish you out."

Elizabeth and Scraps wandered off a ways up the bank, while Cady and James sat in the grass.

"I don't know if that's all there was to it," Cady said.

"All there was to what?"

"Alonzo's bravery." Cady plucked a stem of grass and chewed on it. "The colonel said he was wrestling his own heart. Maybe that's what made him so brave. He was fighting something inside his own self."

James looked out over the sparkling river. "Something inside," he repeated. "I think you may be right,

Cady." He glanced at her. "You know, sometimes you're pretty sharp."

She met his eye, and he felt himself blush. "For a girl," he added hastily.

"Sometimes you are too," she shot back, "for a boy."

The two friends lazed quietly for a while in the shade and cool breezes by the river. Bees hummed over coneflowers, and bluebirds whistled in the branches of aspen and cedars. The sweet-smelling Bear burbled pleasantly. James felt his eyes closing and his head tilting forward.

Next thing he knew, he was wide awake and scrambling to his feet. Scraps had let out several angry, high-pitched barks, and now Elizabeth was shrieking.

James and Cady dashed upstream. Elizabeth hadn't wandered more than a hundred feet, but she was hidden behind a bend in the bank. As they ran toward her, they could hear her screams, more frantic now. Scraps growled and snarled loudly. Even at this distance, they could hear the dog's jaws snapping at something.

A question flashed through James's mind: Who—or what—could it be?

And a number of answers flashed too: Indians, wolves, a bear, a panther . . .

James and Cady rounded the bend. Elizabeth was jumping up and down, yelling, crying, and waving her arms wildly. But she seemed to be unharmed.

Near her was a pile of bleached-white bones, and Scraps rolling around on the riverbank in an odd way, yapping and snarling.

James saw no Indians, or wolves, or bears, or panthers. Not even a coyote.

Then he spotted it. It was coiled near the skull of the buffalo skeleton, its head waving back and forth menacingly.

A rattlesnake!

"Elizabeth!" James screamed. "Get back!"

She was standing not four feet from the rattler. It lunged at her, but Scraps met it in midair, knocking it just below the head. It fell writhing to the ground.

The snake re-coiled and made ready to strike again. Elizabeth ran toward her brother and Cady. James swung her up into his arms and held her tight. She was safe.

But the battle between the little dog and the deadly snake wasn't over yet. Unlike the desperado who'd kicked her off with ease, the snake was Scraps's size. And she wasn't going to let it beat her.

Before James could call off the dog, Scraps lashed out at the rattler, which darted back and returned the parry, once, twice. Scraps dove on top of the snake, gnashing and growling viciously, all flashing teeth and tearing claws.

James watched helplessly as the two animals rolled over and over, the snake wrapping around

Scraps's little body, Scraps biting and snapping in a frenzy.

Then he saw that Scraps had the rattler in her mouth, had it by the back of the neck. The rattler's sharp fangs were useless now. The snake couldn't reach around to sink them into its foe.

Her eyes shut tight, Scraps whipped back and forth, trying to finish the kill. The snake coiled and straightened in an effort to jerk itself free, but Scraps hung on, growling lower now.

At last the snake gave a little shiver and went limp. James set Elizabeth down and ran over to call Scraps off the dead reptile.

His voice was shaky as he called out, "Here, girl! C'mere, girl. You did it, girl."

But it was another ten minutes before Scraps could be persuaded to loosen her jaws from around her attacker's neck.

After much sobbing, and lengthy assurances from James and Cady and Ma that the snake was dead and Scraps was not, Elizabeth explained what had happened.

She'd seen the buffalo skeleton on the bank and decided to take a look. Scraps had been chasing a lizard nearby. When she was examining the skull, all of a sudden she heard a sound like a baby's rattle. Then the head of a snake came slithering through the eyehole of the skull.

She wasn't sure what happened after that. She may have screamed. All she knew was that Scraps was barking and snapping, and that she was afraid Scraps might get hurt. That was when James and Cady came on the scene.

"I told you she was brave," James said to Cady.

"I never said Elizabeth wasn't," she replied.

"You know what I meant." James grinned at Scraps, who was in her usual place in the shade under the wagon. "She took care of that rattler good. If she hadn't been there, Elizabeth might've been killed."

"Jamie," Ma said, "I wasn't for keeping the pup when you first found her, but now I certainly am glad we did."

"Come here, girl," James called Scraps.

Chest puffed out and head held high, Scraps pranced over to him.

"Why, I believe she's *pleased* with herself," Ma said. "You're mighty proud, aren't you, girl?"

Scraps yipped and wagged her tail, and Ma laughed. Then she climbed into the wagon and came out with a long strip of dried buffalo. "Here's a nice reward for the little hero," she said.

She tossed the meat under the wagon. Scraps dived on top of the strip and started gnawing eagerly on one end.

"Well, well, she does like playing the hero," Ma observed, chuckling. "But she likes chewing on the reward even more."

Fifteen

Two Springs

For several days the emigrants hugged the eastern side of the Bear River, traveling northwest. Their plan was to follow the Bear until they got to the Big Bend, where the river curved south. From there the train would venture northwest for about fifty miles through the desolate Portneuf Valley, before reaching Fort Hall on the banks of the Snake.

Pierre Delaroux had taken charge of the Clampson gang. He'd organized a nightly armed watch, and personally saw to it that they behaved during the day. They were kept tied together and hobbled at all times.

Only once, when they refused to keep walking, had Delaroux had to threaten them. His threat consisted of allowing them to do just what they wanted—stop walking. Eleven hours later, parched and on the verge of fainting, the prisoners came stumbling into the nightly circle, begging for water.

After that, the Clampson boys presented no problems.

James was worried about Scott, though. The last time he'd left his family's wagon for any stretch of time was back at Independence Rock. That was weeks ago.

Scott had been frail even at the start of the trip. James recalled how his friend had doubled over coughing from breathing the dusty air in Independence, Missouri, the day they'd met. Mr. Walker had hoped the western air would be good for his son's lungs. But the rigors of the trail had taken a toll on Scott. He was far worse off now than he'd been at the beginning.

At times James wondered if he shouldn't visit his sick friend more often. But it was hard. Mrs. Walker was always right there with him in the wagon, muttering over her Bible. James preferred the company of Cady and Bolt and Scraps.

One afternoon the emigrants formed the nightly circle in a small meadow not far from the Bear. Since gaining South Pass, the emigrants had seen very few Indians. The harsh country west of the Rockies and east of the Bear was as unsuitable for them as it was for the emigrants.

Colonel Stewart had been more vigilant about setting watches and keeping up the circle lately. The train was entering the land of the Snake Indians and the Bannocks, and beyond them were the Cayuses.

None of the western Indians were reputed to be as hostile as were those of the plains. Still, James had heard rumors of bloody massacres. Only a year ago, every living soul at the Whitman Mission, near the Blue Mountains in Oregon, was slaughtered by marauding Indians. Or so people claimed.

After his experiences with the Pawnee, James wasn't quick to believe everything he heard. Still, he didn't like to take chances, and he was glad the colonel was cautious.

Not far from the meadow where the train circled was the famous Soda Springs.

James and Cady were sitting near the Greggs' wagon, eating supper. They were polishing off one little red-flesh trout each. James's pa had hooked them in the Bear. The fish was especially toothsome to James because it was the first game Pa had caught since he'd fallen ill.

"Let's go take a look at the Soda Springs," he suggested.

"That's a fine idea. I haven't had soda water since we left Philadelphia," Cady remarked. "I love the way it tickles my nose."

James was too embarrassed to admit he'd never tasted sparkling water. He wondered what the soda water would feel like bubbling away in his stomach.

"Should we ask Scott to come along?" James said.

Cady's face went serious. "We can ask. I don't

131

know if he'll feel up to it. And even if he does, I don't know that Mother will allow it."

James shrugged. "It's worth a try. Besides, the spring's not far. We could almost carry him there, if we have to." He bit off the crispy tail ends of the trout. He considered the crunchy fins the best part of any fish.

Cady made a face. "How can you eat that? Here." She placed the remains of her fish on his tin plate. "You can have mine too."

James treated himself to seconds, then licked his fingers clean. "Let's go get Scott," he said, getting up. "I believe I'll need a long drink of soda to wash down all these fish spines."

The two friends made their way to the Walkers' wagon. Scott was lying in the darkness of the back, as usual, bundled in blankets.

"Scott?" Cady whispered. "You awake?"

"Course I'm awake," he answered. "It's not even dusk yet."

"You sound good," James said. As his eyes adjusted to the dim light of the wagon's interior, however, he could see that Scott did not look well. His skin shone pale and waxy, and his face was drawn and thin. Dark bluish smudges circled his eyes.

"I'm all right," Scott said.

"You feel up to seeing the Soda Springs?" Cady asked.

"I'd like to see it," Scott admitted. "Help me down."

"Scott . . ." Mrs. Walker said from the front of the wagon.

James waited for her to launch into another of her tirades, but it didn't happen. All she said was "Please don't."

"We'll take care of him, Mother," Cady said gently.

She and James took Scott's arms and eased him over the back panel. But the mere effort of climbing out of the wagon sent Scott into a fit of shallow, wheezing coughs. In seconds he was on his hands and knees, trying to regain his breath.

"Maybe you oughtn't go," James said quietly.

Scott held up his hand and nodded. James wasn't sure if he meant Yes, I can go, or Yes, you're right, I can't go. Either way, James decided his friend was too sick to proceed.

"I hear the spring isn't so special anyhow," James said consolingly. He motioned with his eyes to Cady, and they lifted Scott back into the wagon.

He lay gasping for some time, unable to argue or to thank them. James wasn't sure which was more likely.

Finally Scott was breathing regularly again. "I reckon I'll have to see the spring some other day," he whispered.

"When we come back," Cady said. James noticed tears welling in her eyes. "In 1900," she added.

James felt his own breath catching in his throat. He wiped at his eyes. "Cady and I'll be waiting for you, Scott. You better be there. On Independence Rock, when we're old wrinkled grandparents."

"I'll see you there," Scott said. "Don't you worry. I'll see you. Now you go on. Bring me back a cup of water from the spring."

James dipped his hands into the Soda Springs and brought the water up to his mouth. He slurped some and let it rest on his tongue.

"It burns!" he cried, spitting it out onto the ground nearby.

Cady cackled. "It doesn't *burn,* silly. Those are the bubbles." She knelt down and took a drink. She came up smiling. "Anyone would think you'd never tasted soda water before."

"Of course I have," James snorted.

Cady gave him a sidelong look. He reached down, scooped up more of the sparkling water, and gulped it down. Then he took three more long drafts.

"Mmm," he said. "Just like the soda back home in Pennsyl—*brrrech!*" A shockingly loud belch interrupted his sentence.

Cady laughed, pointing at James's surprised face. "Hoo, hoo! You never *did* taste soda before, did you?"

"Course I did!" James insisted. "I told you I—*brrrrrech!*"

The second belch was so loud it fairly echoed off

134

the mountains in the distance. James slapped his hand over his mouth.

Cady rolled on her back and clutched her stomach, she was laughing so hard. "Look at you!" she crowed gleefully. "You didn't even know soda makes you burp!" Then she let out a small belch of her own. "That's the best part." She cracked up all over again.

So did James, this time.

For the next half hour they guzzled soda water and let fly extravagantly loud burps. Finally they were too bloated with water to take another sip. The burps, however, continued for some time after.

"What do you say we head on up to Steamboat Spring?" James asked during a lull in the croaking.

Cady, too full to speak, nodded.

Steamboat Spring was a little over a mile from Soda Springs. James had been told to look for a low grouping of flattish rocks not far from the trail. Out of these rocks, every few minutes, rose a three-foot geyser of boiling-hot water. The spurting water made a high, piercing whistle like the scape pipe of a steamboat.

The geyser had just begun spouting as James and Cady approached, and they followed the sound to its source.

"Look at that," James said in wonder. "All that water shooting up right out of the ground."

"How do you suppose it got there?" Cady asked.

"Don't know. Rain, I reckon." James frowned. "But how did it get hot?"

"Mother would say it was heated by the devil's flames." Cady wrinkled her nose.

The two friends waited for the geyser to go off again. As they did, James considered Cady's comment about the devil's flames. "You believe some folks really end up in the place down below?" he asked.

"Like that desperado we saw hanging at Fort Laramie?"

"Yeah, like him. And like lots of others who never hanged."

"I don't know," Cady admitted. "It doesn't seem fair to punish a body for all eternity for what they did in one short life on earth. Even desperadoes."

James had never looked at it that way before.

"Why do you ask?" she said.

"Well, I like to think there's a heaven," James explained. "But if there's a heaven for the good souls, there's got to be another place for the bad ones."

Cady shrugged. "We'll all find out in time. For now, we best get back to camp."

The geyser had ceased its spurting, and the sun was edging toward the horizon. James and Cady made their way along the river to camp. They were met there by Mr. Walker.

James knew immediately that something was wrong. Mr. Walker's face looked haggard and drawn, as if his mind was filled with even more worries than usual.

"Cady, James," Mr. Walker began. "I'm glad you got back when you did."

James felt his heart leap into his throat. Though he never believed it would come to this, he knew what was coming before Mr. Walker even said the words.

"What is it, Father?" Cady asked.

"It's Scott, darling." Mr. Walker put his hand on his daughter's shoulder and looked her in the eye. "I'm afraid he won't last the hour."

Sixteen

Seeing the Elephant

James and Cady, along with Mr. Walker, raced to the Walkers' wagon.

A thousand thoughts whirled through James's head. Could Mr. Walker be wrong? Might Scott yet recover? He was a strong person, even if his lungs were weak. Surely he'd live to see Oregon City. But what if Mr. Walker was right? Why did Scott have to die? Why here, why now? Why did it have to be him?

Part of James dreaded what awaited them at the wagon. He didn't want to watch his friend fade away. But he had to be there for him. And for Cady. James was sure Mrs. Walker would be of no comfort to either of her children. She'd be too busy declaiming her awful Bible verses.

James was surprised to find Mrs. Walker up and about. James's ma and the widow Loughery were petting her and murmuring to her, trying to be consoling.

138

Mr. Walker led Cady and James to the wagon. Inside, Scott lay back with his eyes closed. Although the twilight air was quite hot, he was wrapped in blankets. At first James thought he was already dead. Then he noticed his eyelids fluttering a tiny bit.

"Scott?" Cady whispered.

"Howdy, little sister," Scott answered in a thin, rasping voice.

"Not *little* sister," Cady teased. "*Younger* sister."

"You'll always be my little sister," Scott joked. "No matter how big you get." His breath hissed faintly in his lungs. "Did you bring me some soda from the spring?"

"I forgot the canteen," Cady admitted.

"That's all right." Scott lifted his hand, but then let it fall limply onto the blanket. Cady reached into the wagon and held it. "I don't know if I'm up to drinking," he added.

"It wasn't that bubbly anyway," said Cady. "And you'll be well again soon enough."

Scott was silent for a long, long time. Finally he said, "I reckon not, Cady."

James coughed quietly.

"That you, James?"

"Yes, Scott."

"I didn't see you there. I'm glad you're here."

James stood stiffly, fighting back tears. He reminded himself that he had to be strong, for Scott and for Cady.

"I'm glad you're here," Scott repeated. His voice sounded dreamy, as if he was already speaking from some distant, faraway place. "Remember the pact we made on Independence Rock?"

Out of the corner of his eye, James noticed Cady nod.

"I want you two to keep it," Scott continued dreamily. "I like to think of you there in 1900." He paused to catch his breath. "Reading my name and recollecting our days on the trail."

"We'll do it," James said. "We'll keep the pact."

"I know you will," Scott whispered. "And I'll be there when you do. I'll—" He fell into a small coughing fit, lungs whistling like the far-off Steamboat Springs. "I'll be with you."

"You'll always be with me," Cady said. Her voice was strong and clear. "A sister depends on her older brother."

Scott smiled in the darkness of the wagon. "*Big* brother," he said.

"Big brother," Cady agreed.

"And you'll think of me when you're riding Bolt, won't you, James?" he asked.

"Course I will," James said. He knew in his heart that he would never forget his friend.

Mr. Walker came up behind James and Cady, placing his hands on their shoulders. The little group was silent but for the low wheezing of Scott's chest.

"Take care of Mother," Scott said to Cady. "She'll be needing you more than ever."

"I will," she assured him. "Don't you fret. Now you get some rest."

Cady held Scott's hand for a long while. At last Mr. Walker folded his hands around hers and persuaded her to release her brother. He placed her hand in James's, and led them both away.

And so they took their final leave of Scott.

Cady and James sat quietly beneath the Greggs' wagon. They hadn't exchanged a word since parting from Scott. A light rain was falling—the first in weeks.

They spotted Mr. Walker approaching through the mist. Cady tightened her grip on James's hand. She hadn't let go since an hour before.

Mr. Walker squatted next to the wagon. His thinning brown hair was plastered down over his forehead from the damp.

"I'm sorry, Cady," he began. "But your brother departed this life a few minutes ago. He went peacefully, God rest him."

Departed this life. The phrase rang in James's ears. He tried to apply it to his friend, but it didn't take. It wouldn't take. He couldn't accept it. He couldn't believe Scott had actually gone and died.

He was sorry he hadn't spent more time with Scott these last weeks. But with Scott confined to the wagon, and his ma always breathing down his neck . . .

James recalled their first days on the trail, when Scott was healthier, and the adventures they had had together. Trapping a gopher. Watching a herd of buffalo. Carving their names in Independence Rock. Being surrounded by wolves and saved by Indians. James almost smiled to himself. That had been the best one of all—even if they had almost been killed.

And now they would never have any more adventures together.

It was true, James thought, that he'd become closer to Cady than to Scott. But he knew if he lived to be a hundred, when recollecting ox-team days on the Oregon Trail, he'd picture Scott as he'd been back in Independence, Missouri, that very first day—friendly, kind, eager for excitement. James's first friend on the trail.

He felt Cady's grip relax. He wondered what was in her head now. She had a whole lifetime's worth of memories of Scott.

Cady nodded slowly, once. "How is Mother faring?" she asked her father softly.

"Mrs. Gregg and Mrs. Loughery are looking after her." Mr. Walker squinted past James and Cady. "Your mother's a kind woman, James."

"Thank you, sir," James croaked. "I'm sorry about Scott."

Mr. Walker sighed loudly. "She's taking it tolerably well."

James started, then realized Mr. Walker was referring to his own wife, not James's ma.

"I wonder if this might not be a relief to her in some small way," Mr. Walker added. He seemed almost to be talking to himself.

"I'd like to think it will be," Cady said. "For Scott's sake."

James was surprised that she was so calm. As for himself, his whole body trembled. He was fit to burst apart with sorrow. And if he couldn't burst, he was certain he'd collapse in on himself.

"I expect there'll be a service," Cady remarked.

"Colonel Stewart was kind enough to offer to say a few words." Mr. Walker crawled under the wagon and put his arm around his daughter. "How are you, my darling girl?"

Cady let go of James's hand at long last. She began to say something, but only a small sound rose from her throat. She buried her face in her father's chest and wept silently.

James stared into the misty rain and swallowed hard over and over again to keep the tears down.

Early next morning Colonel Stewart held his plumed hat to his chest and surveyed the mourners. They were assembled in a clearing near a stand of aspen. A breeze rustled the leaves and swayed the white trunks.

At the head of the freshly dug grave was a small,

blackish rock. Etched into one side was a cross, and under it the words:

SCOTT WALKER
B. FEB. 22, 1835
D. AUG. 15, 1848

James gripped his elbows and shivered in the cool morning air. On one side of him was his family—Jeremy, Elizabeth, Pa, and Ma. On the other were the Walkers—Cady and her parents. Will and Sara were there too, as were most of the other emigrants.

James was comforted by the presence of his loved ones. But he couldn't stop shaking at the thought of Scott in the cold, still earth. He'd seen other burials on the trail, but this one was different. This one was his friend's.

Colonel Stewart stepped forward. "We gather here this solemn morn to mark the passing of our own Scott Walker—loyal son of John and Rebecca, loving brother of Cady. A young man uncomplaining in life and fearless in death."

The colonel paused thoughtfully, then continued. "All know the western way is fraught with hardship and peril—life and death, misery and joy entwined like the trail itself. So it is for young and old alike.

"When faced with tragedy, old-timers like myself say that we've seen the elephant. Seeing the elephant—God's most awesome creation, embodiment of all the forces mortal man can never comprehend.

"In every person's life the elephant must needs appear. The time will come to each mortal soul when God or fate decrees a sudden dire anguish. For many of us that time is now."

The colonel paused again, and James considered his words. Seeing the elephant. James had, in fact, never seen one. He pictured a huge, shaggy, monstrous beast, all long white teeth and flappy ears, horrible to behold. To see the elephant was to wrestle with fear, to grapple with sorrow. To fight something inside. James knew he was seeing the elephant now.

"Some of you may recall," Colonel Stewart said, "the story of Alonzo Tanner. Like Scott Walker, whom we honor today, he fought a battle he knew he could not win. Thus was his courage measured, and thus he was the bravest man I ever knew. Alonzo Tanner was not, however, the bravest *person* I ever knew."

James was surprised to hear that. Who could possibly be braver than Alonzo Tanner?

"The bravest person I ever knew," said the colonel, "was Pocalalla, Alonzo Tanner's bride. For shortly after he won her from her father the chief, Alonzo Tanner fell ill and died.

"A brave thing it is indeed to meet one's end with courage. But far, far braver are those who must survive the loss.

145

"Pocalalla mourned her true love, for all her days. In the same manner have I grieved for my own dear departed wife. Pocalalla never forgot nor ceased to love Alonzo Tanner, as I still love and honor Dorothy. And as you will love Scott to your last hour.

"And yet Pocalalla persevered, with stout heart and generous hand, to live and breathe, and make joy upon this earth, until the Great Spirit her maker called her to Alonzo Tanner in the sky.

"And so we—John, Rebecca, Cady, all of us— must do as the brave Indian maid did, and carry on as Scott would have us. Not full of despair, but full of hope. Not with hearts burdened by sorrow, but with hearts rejoicing in expectation of the good Lord's mercy and wisdom."

The colonel bowed his head, and James joined in the brief prayer that followed. After the Amen, James's ma commenced singing in her clear soprano an old, familiar hymn. Soon all the mourners merged their voices in the melody. The lovely final verse went:

> "While I draw this fleeting breath,
> When mine eyelids close in death,
> When I rise to worlds unknown
> And behold Thee on Thy throne,
> Rock of Ages, cleft for me,
> Let me hide myself in Thee."

Seventeen

Fort Hall

Within the hour, the emigrants were on the trail again. There was no occasion, not even a burial, that could delay the train for even a day.

James trudged beside the family wagon in a daze. Without so much as a second look, he passed the two springs he'd visited with Cady the day before.

Not three miles farther on, the Bear River swung to the south at its Big Bend. There the main trail left the river and continued northwest, through the dusty Portneuf Valley. About thirty miles distant lay the Snake River and Fort Hall.

At the Big Bend of the Bear, however, a smaller trail, called the Hudspeth Cutoff, forked off toward California. The cutoff skirted the Great Salt Desert before joining up with the main California Trail, which diverged from the Oregon Trail thirty miles beyond Fort Hall.

147

At the head of the train, Colonel Stewart and Pierre Delaroux didn't hesitate for a moment when they reached the fork to the Hudspeth Cutoff. The colonel waved his arm to the right, and the lead wagon started toward Oregon City.

Immediately James saw Mr. McElroy gallop past. He was hailing the colonel, as if he wanted to discuss something. Soon afterward, the train came to a halt. Only the first three wagons had passed the fork in the road.

James, Jeremy, and Pa trotted to the front of the train to see what the delay was about. By now most of the other emigrants, along with Colonel Stewart and Pierre Delaroux, had gathered there too.

"I hear tell there's streams in California so sparkly with gold, you have to squint to look at them," Mr. McElroy was saying.

"Nuggets the size of your thumb," added Mr. Batkin. He held up his own to illustrate.

Mr. Skonecki nodded vigorously. "The men are rich, like kings, in California," he asserted.

Pierre Delaroux grinned at the men from atop his big brown horse. "Oh, yes, every man a king in California! Gold nuggets too big to lift!" He burst out laughing. "My foolish friends, do you not know tales, fables, lies when you hear them?" He shook his head. "Come, too much folly will slow us. Oregon awaits." He heeled his horse and trotted away.

"I reckon he's right," said Mr. McElroy. "Those're

148

just stories. Best to go on to Oregon, like we planned."

Several of the other men nodded in agreement.

Then Eli Meacham spoke up. "Has your Mr. Delaroux ever been to California? Does he know them stories is false, or does he just want to be certain we don't get there to find out different?"

James shook his head in disgust. Mr. Meacham seemed to think everyone was as low-down and tricky as he was.

"Why would Mr. Delaroux not want you to go to California?" Colonel Stewart asked. It was the same question James had.

"It don't take much figuring," Mr. Meacham said. "Delaroux knows the north country. That's why we hired him to take us to Oregon. But if ever'one wanted to go to California, where he ain't never been, he'd be out of a job."

James thought that was about the silliest notion he'd ever heard. Several of the men started voicing their objections, too.

"Or maybe Delaroux wants to make sure we all go to Oregon," Mr. Meacham went on, "so there's less competition for him when he goes to California."

"That is nonsense, sir," said Colonel Stewart. "Pierre Delaroux is a trapper and guide, not a miner. And you folks are farmers. If you know what's good for you, you will forget about California and set your mind on planting crops and raising cows in Oregon. Finding gold is a fool's dream."

Most of the men agreed with the colonel's words. But James knew some were not convinced, including Jeremy. James overheard him talking with Mr. McElroy about where the best panning streams were rumored to be.

Finally Mr. Meacham declared, "There's gold in California, and I aims to find it. Now I'm taking the cut-off. Any man with gumption enough is welcome to join me. All you others will live to regret your mistake."

Mr. Meacham strode back to his wagon, near the end of the train. He called to his oxen and cracked the whip over their heads. Steering them around the wagons in front of him, he took the left-hand fork, along the Hudspeth Cutoff.

In the back of the wagon sat his wife. James wondered what she thought of her husband's decision. She didn't look pleased, that was for sure.

Not a man moved to join them.

"You can't go alone, Mr. Meacham," Colonel Stewart called after him. "You'll never make it. It's too dangerous."

"I'll make it, all right!" he yelled back. "And when I'm rich, maybe I'll hire one or two of you to be my bootblacks." He cackled loudly. "Or maybe I won't!" He cracked the whip again, and within minutes disappeared around an outcropping of rock.

James had to admit to himself that he was glad to see Mr. Meacham go. He wondered if he would ever learn of his enemy's fate.

Colonel Stewart simply shook his head and addressed the remaining men. "You fellows, return to your wagons. We have another ten miles to roll today."

Fort Hall, on the banks of the Snake River, was a disappointment. Even by the standards of western outposts, it was shabby, slight, and mean. There was only one building, and it was made of dried mud.

Still, the emigrants were glad to be camped outside it. The trail through the Portneuf Valley had been slow going. Long stretches of road had been covered with sand six inches deep. They'd had to ford numerous streams before following the Portneuf River for several miles. And after the river, there'd been a high ridge to cross, then more sand and more creeks.

Finally, three days after leaving the Hudspeth Cutoff behind, the weary emigrants had rolled up to Fort Hall. There Colonel Stewart handed over the Clampson brothers to agents of the Hudson Bay Company, the trapping outfit that maintained the fort.

James was happy to be rid of the desperadoes. Though he trusted Pierre Delaroux to keep them captive, he hadn't felt safe with them near.

James didn't relish the thought of the Clampsons' fate. He knew what fur companies did with desperadoes in their territory. And he didn't want to be party to it any more than he already was. Seeing one man hanged at Fort Laramie had been quite enough for him.

151

Cady had been spending less time with the Greggs since Scott died. As her father and she had hoped, Mrs. Walker was actually behaving less strangely. She still read her Bible, but not as loudly. And now she sometimes read nice passages. Her son's death seemed to be as much a release for her as it had been for Scott.

Gold in California was the talk of the train. Despite Colonel Stewart and Delaroux's efforts, many of the men had succumbed to gold fever. The trappers, traders, and soldiers assembled at Fort Hall had gold on their minds too. They further fed the emigrants' fantasies. Only James's pa, Mr. Walker, Mr. Jennington, and Mr. Teague were immune to it.

James and Jeremy were lounging in the grass near the wagon. James was tossing a stick to Scraps, who had learned to fetch. Jeremy was writing a letter.

"Howdy, boys," Will hailed them, pulling up on his horse. "Want to come with me to the fort?"

"Maybe some other time," James answered. He didn't want to stumble upon any more necktie parties.

"Some other time?" Will jumped off his mount. "When do you plan to be back?"

James shrugged. "I've seen enough of forts. You go ahead, though."

"Jeremy?" Will said. "You want to come?"

Jeremy looked up. "What do you think of this? It's to Missy." He read carefully from the letter he was writing: "'If possible I would fain take eagle's

152

wings and spend the day with you.' Too fancy?"

James thought so, but he didn't say anything.

"That's right good," Will assured Jeremy. "Girls appreciate a noble sentiment."

"I thought she'd like it," said Jeremy. "I hear tell you can send a letter from Fort Hall. The traders have messengers running back east by way of the Canadian colonies. I'm letting Missy know what my plans are."

"And what are they?" Will asked.

Jeremy shot James a look. "Soon as we get to Oregon City, I'm packing up and heading south to California," he said. "I'm going to make my fortune and send for Missy."

James was astonished. How could his brother say that? How could he sit there and admit to betraying the family?

"That sounds like a good plan." Will flopped down in the grass beside them. "I was thinking I'd head for California too."

"What?" James exploded. "But why? I thought you wanted to start up a little farm in Oregon, where the people are free. Why would you want to go chasing after gold?"

"Jamie," he replied, "a farmer's wife labors from sun to sun. Look at your own ma, how hard she works. Sara will never be able to do that now. Thanks to me," he added bitterly.

Before James could object, Will went on. "I reckon

153

I'll go to California and stake a claim to the richest mineral ore in the territory. Then Sara will never have to work again. We'll have a big house, like my daddy's plantation back home, and a hundred servants to wait on her."

"I thought you didn't want servants," James muttered. He didn't like what the thought of gold did to his brother, or to Will. "I thought that's why you left Virginia in the first place."

"Oh, I'll *pay* my servants," Will explained. "And they'll be free to leave anytime they want."

Jeremy nodded approvingly. "Missy and I'll be neighbors with you."

Will grinned. "In the mansion next door." He turned to James, and his voice went serious. "Jamie, you have to understand. It's my fault Sara was injured. I have to make it up to her. I just have to." Then he turned back to Jeremy. "Let's deliver that letter."

He and Jeremy mounted the horse and rode off toward the fort.

James was certain Will was wrong. Sara didn't want to be rich. She didn't think Will owed her anything. It wasn't like her to feel that way. But James didn't know how to convince Will that he was mistaken.

EIGHTEEN

THE VALLEY SO SWEET

Talk of gold was all James had heard in the three days since the emigrants had left Fort Hall. Several men said they wished they'd accompanied Eli Meacham along the Hudspeth Cutoff. When they reached the fork to the main California Trail, these same men claimed, they were heading south.

The train was following the rim of Snake River canyon now. Hundreds of feet below, at the bottom of the gorge, lay Bannock Indian villages. The Bannocks lived in round huts, called wickiups, made of matted brush and bark lashed over wood frames. Like the tepees of the Dakota Indians, wickiups were shaped like cones, and usually had trails of smoke rising out of the peaks.

James admired the way the Indians used the different resources available to them. In the plains, where the buffalo were numerous and the trees were

155

few, the Dakota and Pawnee made their houses out of buffalo hides. Here, where the buffalo were scarce and the trees plentiful, the Bannocks made their houses out of wood.

During nooning, four Bannocks approached. James was watering Bolt and playing with Scraps when he saw them coming. He quickly tied Bolt to a picket and whistled Scraps into the wagon.

Many of the men in the train had already reached for their rifles—just in case. But the Bannocks had come only to trade, and the men put away their guns.

"We going to meet them?" James asked his pa.

"We'll take a look at what they have," he answered. "Meantime, help me dig the fishhooks out of the wagon."

The day before they'd left Independence, Missouri, Pa had bought twelve-dozen fishhooks. James couldn't imagine why his family would need so many. Then Pa explained the hooks would be valuable as barter in the Snake River country. And now, sure enough, their time had come.

James ran to fetch Cady. She and her mother were in their wagon, sewing quietly. It had been a long time since James had seen Mrs. Walker looking so peaceful. He wondered whether, when Cady lost her brother, she'd gained her mother back. That was almost too much to hope for.

He decided he'd better not ask Mrs. Walker if Cady could go with him to trade with the Indians. It was better not to disturb them. They seemed happy together, for once.

Pa and James met the Bannocks in a clearing not far from the train. Pa told his son that the Indians were offering pouches full of dried salmon roe.

James knew that a salmon was a big pink fish of the western waters. But he didn't know what the roe could be. He'd always thought roe was another word for deer. At least that's what it was back in Pennsylvania.

Pa counted out ten fishhooks to one of the Bannocks and was handed a small bag in exchange. James opened the bag and looked inside. It was filled with what looked like shriveled red berries.

"We're going to eat these?" he asked his pa.

" 'Deed we are," Pa said. "I hear they're tasty."

James pinched a few between his thumb and forefinger and placed them on his tongue.

"Bleh! Salty!" he exclaimed, chewing quickly and swallowing. "What part of the fish are they, anyway?"

"Why, Jamie, they aren't *part* of the fish at all," Pa said.

James looked at him blankly.

"They're roe. Eggs. Fish eggs."

Dried fish eggs! Why hadn't anyone warned him? He wanted to clear his mouth and spit on the ground, but he knew his pa would be angry with him if he did. It would be insulting to the Indians, too.

"These fellows"—Pa indicated the Bannocks—"know where the spawning places in the river are. Let me have a taste." He reached in the pouch, put some roe in his mouth, and chewed quickly. "Right savory, I'd say," he pronounced, smiling.

"Right salty, I'd say," James grumbled.

Well, he thought, they'd cost only ten fishhooks. There were one hundred and thirty-four more to go. He just hoped his pa wouldn't trade them for more dried salmon roe.

That afternoon the train reached the fork to the California Trail. Rather than force the emigrants to decide immediately which road they wanted to take, Colonel Stewart rounded the wagons into the nightly circle.

"I've heard enough talk the last few days," Colonel Stewart addressed the emigrants, "to know that some of you have decided to head south."

No one spoke. James noticed a number of men—Mr. McElroy, Mr. Batkin, Mr. Skonecki—staring intently at their shoes.

"I won't try to convince you you're making a mistake," the colonel continued. "You already know my thoughts on the matter. But I do want you to know that there will be no hard feelings among those of us who are going to Oregon. I'm sure I speak for everyone when I wish you Godspeed." The colonel doffed his big plumed hat and waved it in the air.

158

"May you find your fortune in California as we find ours in Oregon."

Several men, including Mr. McElroy and the others who'd been looking at their shoes, applauded the colonel's generous words.

Then Pa dug his fiddle out of the wagon. He was joined by Mr. Smoot, and by Mr. Moss on the concertina. But the emigrants weren't in the mood for dancing. They knew that on the morn they'd be parting, some never to meet again.

Soon the musicians were taking requests for slow, sweet tunes, the sadder the better. The sun set and the stars condensed out of the black sky. Folks hummed along with the fiddles or sang quietly, while the birds called in the distance and the echo of a coyote's howl rose out of the Snake River canyon.

A feeling was rising in James, and the feeling was a dull, aching sadness. He had never felt such a sorrow, not even when Scott died. And he couldn't even say why.

He went to search for Sara. Seeing her now was like pressing on a loose tooth—it hurt, but he couldn't help himself.

She was sitting on an upturned barrel, her bad leg propped out at an odd angle. James sat in the dirt beside her. "Where's Will?"

"He's off talking to the men about California." She smiled weakly at him. "That's all he ever talks about now."

159

James nodded. "He wants to find gold."

"I know." Sara looked pained. "He's burning to go to California. He'd like to leave with the others tomorrow. But he can't. And it's I who's holding him back. He'd be free to strike it rich if it weren't for me."

"But, Sara," James said, "Will doesn't care about gold. He wants to be rich for your sake. To take care of you."

"That's nice of you to say, Jamie."

"I'm not just saying it. It's true."

Sara ruffled his hair. "You're sweet."

James blushed fiercely.

"But you're young yet," she added. "Will's wild, untamed. When he wanted to go west, he didn't let himself be tied down by his daddy's plantation. And now that he wants to go to California, he shouldn't be tied down by . . ." Her voice cracked. "By a cripple," she finished bitterly. She blinked rapidly and dabbed at her eyes with her handkerchief. "Someday you'll understand."

"Will's not like that," James insisted. "He loves you."

Sara smiled through her tears at him, and his heart fairly melted away. But it was clear she didn't believe him. He wondered if Sara would ever again be confident of Will's love. It was a thought that made him sadder than ever.

James headed across the circle, toward his own wagon. In the dim light of a campfire, he spotted

Cady and her mother sitting together near their wagon. Mrs. Walker had her arms wrapped around her daughter. Cady's eyes were shut, and her face was peaceful.

Wonders never cease! James thought. Perhaps he had judged Mrs. Walker too harshly. He couldn't imagine what it was like to watch your son, your own flesh and blood, suffer day after day and then die before your eyes.

He'd been sure that Scott's death would be the final blow to Mrs. Walker's sanity. Rather, it had seemed to lift a great weight off her. And Cady was obviously delighted to have her back.

And still the feeling was with him. Why did he feel so sad this night? James wondered.

He stopped by to check on Bolt and Scraps. The little dog, asleep beneath the wagon, was already looking fatter. James smiled at the thought of how well her name suited her. That very evening she'd gobbled up the dried salmon roe left over on James's plate.

Bolt was eating plenty too. His shiny coat was proof of it. James slapped his flank, and the horse neighed long and deeply.

Then James heard the tune of a familiar song, his pa playing the melody, his ma singing harmony above it. The first verse went:

"There's not in this wide world a valley so sweet
As the vale in whose bosom the bright waters meet.

161

The last ray of feeling, even life, shall depart
Ere the bloom of that valley shall fade from my heart."

Where had he heard the song before? James cast his mind back, searching. And now it came to him. He'd learned it long ago, when he lived on a little farm in Pennsylvania.

James started. Long ago? Less than six months ago they'd left Franklin. But it seemed like a lifetime, a lifetime of new experiences and adventures, of comings and goings.

Tomorrow he'd hail farewell to Mr. Batkin, and to Mr. Skonecki, and maybe even to Mr. Sundstrom, who had the wisest oxen this side of Bethlehem. The train was breaking up. And when those emigrants still heading for their original destination got to Oregon City, they would all go their separate ways. James might never see many of them again.

He would surely never again see the shadowed valley where he was born, where he spent the years of his childhood. The western trail led to a new life, but it also led away from an old one.

On the trail, every day was filled with walking. And every step toward Oregon left something or someone behind. The little farm outside Franklin. The mighty buffalo of the plains. The numberless passenger pigeons of the Rockies. Little Jasper Smoot, buried in a burned-out hillside. Scott. And now all these others.

162

Finally James understood why he felt so sad, so sorrowful, on this night of farewells. The last verse of the song, splitting the night air and rising toward the stars, gave the answer:

"'Twas that friends, the beloved of my bosom, were near,
Who made every scene of enchantment more dear.
And who has felt how the best charms of nature improve
When we see them reflected from looks that we love?"

James cherished those close to him more than ever that night. Between here and Oregon City lay sandy deserts, swift rivers, and jagged mountain peaks. He knew there would be more partings, more sorrow before he could call Oregon home.

Yet he knew, too, that every day he took one step closer to being a man.

Here's a scene from the next
book in this exciting trilogy,
Over the Rugged Mountain. . . .

James trotted Bolt along the narrow, stony path. The rifle lay across his lap.

"Why do you get to ride while I'm walking?" Cady asked him sharply.

"Because Bolt's my horse, not yours," he answered. "Besides, I told you I didn't want you along on this hunt. You're just going to scare the game off."

"I didn't last time," she argued.

"No, but you didn't manage to hit anything, either," James replied. "And there were jackrabbits everywhere."

"That was my first hunt," Cady sniffed. "I'm sure I'm a better shot now. Anyway, your pa said I could come."

"And that's the only reason I'm letting you stay with me," James muttered testily. "Now, hurry up. You're walking too slow."

"I'm going as fast as I can," Cady said. "The air's so thin, it's hard to get a good breath."

They were crossing Devil's Half Acre, a treacherous pass almost a mile up in the Cascade Range. Even Bolt was breathing heavily.

James sucked in as much cold clean air as he could through his nostrils. It smelled of pine sap and fir needles. All around him the giant trees sprang out of the rocky floor. The scrub brush below them was twisted into fantastic shapes by the wind.

He'd never seen anything like Devil's Half Acre—the huge pinecones scattered among the boulders, the immense jagged stumps of trees that had fallen over with age. It was nothing like the soft misty valley back in Pennsylvania where he'd grown up.

James knew he had to put the past behind him. He was in Oregon now—Oregon City itself was less than fifty miles away. And despite the strangeness of the land, it was already feeling like home.

"Slow down, James!" Cady called.

He turned Bolt around. Cady was trailing him by a good fifty feet now. She plodded heavily up the trail, her shoulders slouched, her chest heaving.

"Deer aren't going to wait all day for us," he yelled gleefully. "Get a move on, tortoise girl."

"I'm coming, I'm coming," Cady hollered. "If you think I'm going so slow, why don't you walk for a while?"

" 'Cause I'm smart enough to be riding a horse," James shouted back. He dropped Bolt's reins and crossed his arms impatiently. The rifle was balanced across the horn of his saddle.

Suddenly he felt Bolt stiffen beneath him. The horse's ears flattened against its skull. Something was wrong.

"James!" Cady yelled. "There's a—"

Her cry was cut off by a piercing scream.

Bolt started. It was all James could do to grab the reins with one hand and wheel the horse around.

Now James's heart raced. He and Bolt were face-to-face with a snarling panther crouched on a rocky ledge not ten feet above them. James stared into the big yellow eyes of the angry cat.

It raised its heavy whiskered lips over its long white fangs and hissed. The muscles in its shoulders were bunched and ready to spring. Its golden tail twitched rhythmically.

James fumbled for the rifle, then realized it had fallen off his lap when he'd spun around.

The panther howled again, chilling James to the bone.

Bolt reared, and James grabbed onto his mane to keep from being thrown. He patted Bolt's neck and made shushing noises to soothe him. The panther was sure to spring at any sudden movement. But without the rifle, James was defenseless against the big cat. All he and Bolt could do was hope for mercy.

166

He glanced back at Cady. She was frozen in her tracks just twenty feet away.

"Run, Cady!" he shouted. "Run!"

The panther let out another piercing scream. To James it seemed as if all the devils in the underworld had made their way to this one little half acre in the Cascades.

Cady remained stock-still.

"Cady, run!" he urged.

The hairs on the back of his neck stood on end as the panther growled.

"Now!"

Cady met his eyes and held his gaze for an instant. She winked coolly.

Then she darted for the gun.

1 (800) I LUV BKS!

If you'd like to hear more about your
favorite young adult novels and writers . . .
OR
If you'd like to tell us what you thought
of this book or other books
you've recently read . . .

CALL US at 1(800) I LUV BKS
[1(800) 458-8257]

Monday to Friday, 9AM – 8PM EST

You'll hear a new message about books and
other interesting subjects each month.

**The call is free, but please get
your parents' permission first.**